DEAR YVETTE . . .

nobody thinks more about death than I do, Yvette. Don't you realize that you and I are going to end up in a coffin soon enough? Can't we at least be friends before our time comes? If you'd only give me a chance. You're probably saying to yourself "Why me?" again. Well, I have a feeling about you. I have a feeling you're a very special individual. I have a vision that in some weird and bizarre way you and I have a destiny with each other. Could we go out Friday night? Please answer me. I'm going to send you flowers or candy every day until you do. Let's be friends, Yvette, before it's too late.

Sincerely yours,
Dewey Daniels

Bantam Books by Paul Zindel
Ask your bookseller for the books you have missed

THE EFFECT OF GAMMA RAYS ON MAN-IN-THE-MOON
   MARIGOLDS
I NEVER LOVED YOUR MIND
MY DARLING, MY HAMBURGER

I Never Loved Your Mind

Paul Zindel

BANTAM BOOKS · TORONTO · NEW YORK · LONDON

*This low-priced Bantam Book
has been completely reset in a type face
designed for easy reading, and was printed
from new plates. It contains the complete
text of the original hard-cover edition.*
NOT ONE WORD HAS BEEN OMITTED.

RL 6, IL 9-up

I NEVER LOVED YOUR MIND
*A Bantam Book / published by arrangement with
Harper & Row, Publishers*

PRINTING HISTORY
Harper & Row edition published May 1970

	Bantam edition / February 1972	
2nd printing .... February 1972	6th printing .... May 1975
3rd printing .... December 1972	7th printing .... December 1976
4th printing .... July 1973	8th printing .... June 1977
5th printing .... June 1974	9th printing ...... February 1978
10th printing .... January 1979	

ISBN 0-553-12774-8

Published simultaneously in the United States and Canada

PRINTED IN THE UNITED STATES OF AMERICA

To URSULA

I Never Loved
Your Mind

Chapter 1

If you knew I was a seventeen-year-old handsome guy hacking out this verbose volume of literary ecstasy, you'd probably think I was one of those academic genii who run home after a titillating day at school, panting to commence cello lessons. I regret to inform you, however, that I do not suffer from scholasticism of the brain. In fact, I suffer from it so little I dropped out of my puerile, jerky high school exactly eleven months ago.

About the only thing I do remember from that academic abyss is my English teacher, Mrs. Konlan, saying, when she was sober, that if you're going to write anything you can't just say nasty things all the time. You're supposed to say nice things too so the story will be richer—*more balanced*, she'd say. Well, I don't totally agree with that. I think it might make this book crap. (I use the latter term as a shortened version of the term *crapulous*, which your dictionary will tell you means *intemperate*.) But the point is I have no intention of allowing my sincere straight-from-the-coronary gushing of artistic purity to be interfered with, so if any special balancing has to be done, I'll just do that in footnotes. Also, if I think of anything absolutely too crass or mundane, I'll shove that down there too. Look at the bottom of this page and you'll get the idea, unless you're retarded.* And you might as well know now this is not one of those stories where you're supposed to forget you're reading a book and get unctuously involved in the plot. I know it's a book and you know it's a book, so let's just both of us admit it's a book. Of course, if you insist on making believe it's not a book you're holding, I don't mind either. Make believe you're holding a baby-bulldog's behind for all I care.

Now what I've got to tell you begins about three months ago when I started working at this penicillin pleasure palace called Richmond Valley Hospital. On that fateful first day of my employment a mean lady† in personnel had me fill out pension and social security forms, plus a lot of other flotsam and jetsam. Then she sent me to meet my boss, Mr. Donaldson, who was the big cheese in the inhalation-therapy department. The first couple of things he said almost made me engage in reverse peristalsis, but I told myself what the hell. That's what I do any time something disturbs me. I just say what the hell.

"Now, Dewey, you seem like a bright young man. I'll bet you already know the formula for a molecule of oxygen."

"Yes, sir."

"Well?"

"O_2."

"I knew you did."

He kept grinning at me, a shriveled smile swinging at the base of his skinny bald head. It was like talking

---

* Mrs. Konlan was merely rumored to partake of an occasional double bourbon before breakfast. It was also thought she was moonlighting as a go-go dancer.

† She reminded me of a tomboy from grammar school by the name of Jeanette Matischewitz, whom all the boys used to applaud whenever she jumped out of an apple tree because she had holes in her pants.

to a thin, short lustreless forty-five-year-old Easter egg. And the inhalation-therapy-department office looked as though someone had chopped off one-eighth of a Chock Full O'Nuts coffeehouse. It had so many glass windows the first thing that crossed my mind was that if an over-passionate nurse or candy-striper* tried to attack me, it'd be as private as being raped in Bombay during rush hour.

"Why did you leave school?" Donaldson asked.

"I wasn't learning anything."

"Oh?"

"I could've gotten nineties in everything if I'd wanted to, but they weren't teaching anything urgent."

"What do you consider urgent, Dewey?" he inquired, with just the right accent on *urgent* so we'd both know he totally understood the blind folly of youth.

"Well," I said, "let me tell you what I consider *non*-urgent. First, like Madagascar. I don't think it's urgent that I know exactly what the imports and exports of Madagascar are. And I wasn't interested in the state, color, odor, solubility, or density of bromine. And in math they were teaching pi r-squared for the twenty-third time."

"I see."

There was a frantic banging on the door behind me, and I turned to see a girl peering through the glass. As she opened the door her popping eyes made her look like an owl with a thyroid condition.

"Excuse me, Mr. Donaldson," came this high, piercing voice, "the man in room four twenty-three is—"

"Can't you see I'm in conference?" Donaldson bellowed.

---

* Candy-stripers are high-school volunteers. The ones at Richmond Valley Hospital were all revered except for Marjorie Lou Simonson, who used to curse so much she was nicknamed Tommy Toilet-Tongue.

The girl's eyes deflated. She gritted her teeth, and for a moment it looked like she was going to spit at the cranky old Easter egg. "But—"

"You heard me!" Donaldson roared again. Then in a calmer voice he added, "I'll be with you in a minute. Just wait your turn." He looked at me and flashed a go-on-with-what-you-were-saying smile.

I cleared my throat.

"Every time I asked a question I was interested in, the teachers told me to shut up."

"For example?"

"Embalming."

"*Embalming?*"

"Why do we really embalm? I think one of the major reasons is to make sure that anybody who ends up in a coffin doesn't sit up during the wake."*

Donaldson rearranged himself in his chair. He opened his mouth but didn't say anything. Then he turned to the girl, who was still squealing near the door.

"All right. What do you want?"

"Well," she started again with her ultrasonic voice, "I really thought it might be of passing interest to you that the man in room four twenty-three is turning blue."

"What?"

"Mr. Thiebold is turning blue."

"Where's the nurse?"

"On a coffee break."

"Oh, my God!"

He bolted out of his chair as he finally realized what the girl had said. By now so much blood had rushed to his head he looked like a maroon Easter egg.

"Get the bird!" he screamed at me. "Get the bird!"

---

* I've heard a lot of rich people in California refuse to be embalmed and insist that a telephone be buried with them in the coffin.

"What bird?" I inquired.

"That *bird!*" He pointed to a corner of the office, rotated one hundred and eighty degrees, and started flinging open cabinet doors. "Roll it to four twenty-three!"

I looked where he had pointed, expecting to see a giant cockatoo on wheels.

"*This*," the girl said as though directing an idiot.

A moment later I was pushing a phantasmagorically morose contraption down the hall, with the owl-eyed girl leading the way. I finally noticed the metallic script of a brand name on the machine: *BYRD*.

"In *here.*" The girl stopped outside one of the rooms. I tried to manipulate the cart through the door, but the front right wheel wouldn't turn. With a kick, the girl set it right and pulled the cart suddenly. I practically fell on my face. Everything was happening so imbecilely I thought I was having one of those nightmares I used to have during puberty after eating a pound of pepperoni before retiring. Red lights were flashing up and down the corridor. I looked behind me and saw Donaldson charging forth, followed by two nurses. To get out of the way of the oncoming brigade, I moved into the room. What I saw in the bed made me wish I had fled the other way. This old prune of a man in an oxygen tent was staring right at me with his mouth hanging open, making a wheezing sound. He was blue all right. The only guy I ever saw bluer was in a cinematic religious extravaganza where a pagan potentate had one of his slaves painted blue to seal his sweat pores and then made him dance until he croaked in his own poisons.

The girl swung the machine into position. Then Donaldson and the nurses barged in, and I stood against the far wall.

"Roll the tent back," Donaldson ordered.

The nurses obliged, and he reached under the sparkling transparency and loosened the patient's pajama

5

top. Suddenly a large man* in a white jacket moved, pantherlike, into the room. I was so confused I found myself staring for about ten seconds at the gigantic crepe-soled shoes this new guy was wearing. By the time I looked up from the floor, he was tapping the prune's throat and the wheezing seemed to be growing wilder. He said something softly to the nurses, who instantly flew into action. One began running water into the sink, and the other placed two bottles on a white towel which covered the bed stand. I moved closer as the doctor hovered farther and farther over the bed. He swabbed the center of the patient's neck with some cotton dipped in alcohol. As if from nowhere a scalpel appeared in his right hand, its glistening edge disappearing into the spectacularly blue throat. At the first sight of blood gushing from the neck I felt my knees go out from under me.

_____

* He had a stethoscope sticking out of one pocket, and so much dandruff he looked like a vanilla-ice-cream cone that had just been dipped in albino sprinkles.

Chapter 2

I remember regaining consciousness* and still thinking I was unconscious because when I opened my
eyes, I couldn't see anything. It took me a minute of
blinking before I realized I was staring at a white ceiling. Anybody else would have been relieved they
hadn't croaked, but I let out a scream. It was a little,
manly scream, like the kind an actor lets out when
he's playing the movie role of an archeologist who
pooh-poohs the mummy's curse but the mummy gets
him anyway. I knew I was looking at a white ceiling,
but I was scared because the thought crossed my
mind that maybe that's what death was—one big
white glossy ceiling.

"Shut up," came a treble voice.

I propped myself up on my elbows. The owl-girl
was standing in front of a cabinet on the other side of
the room. My enormous cerebrum then begin to per-
ceive it was in some grotesque chamber—stark walls

---

* I only passed out once before in my life, and that was last
summer when I was bombed at Lake George and went water-
skiing at midnight with a lantern in my teeth.

and gaping sinks and squatting pressure cookers.*

"Where am I?" I asked, so astounded at the un-original remark I felt like cauterizing my tongue.

"The autopsy room."

My lower jaw flipped down, and I think she was afraid I was going to pass out again.

"The other rooms were occupied," she added quickly.

I tried to sit up, but she rushed over and, with a hand on my chest, pushed me back down.

"Donaldson wants you to rest."

"I don't feel like resting."

"Lie still."

I gyrated my head to see what I was lying on. It was one of those cots on wheels, and for a minute I thought it was some gizmo for moving corpses.

"Is this for stiffs?"

"No."

I started to let out a heavy sigh but changed it half-way to a deep breath, not particularly recognizable as an expression of relief. The girl stood over me a moment longer, then returned to her position across the room. I raised my head onto a pillow to see her better.

"It's weird," she said.

"What?"

"A while ago you mentioned embalming. Now look where you are."

I didn't answer.

"I'm not making fun of you. I was involved in what you were saying to Donaldson." She sat down on a high metal stool and reached into a pocket of her uniform.

"Would you like half a broccoli sandwich?"

"No, thank you," I replied, not allowing my voice to

---

* The room smelled like one of those preserved grasshoppers they always give you to dissect in high-school bio. I liked bio, and I often remember things from it, like how the female praying mantis bites off the head of the male praying mantis after sex.

8

betray the slight dose of nutritional horror I felt watching her unwrap her little snack.

She took a hideous bite and began munching along with a rolling-of-the-eyes bit, like how tasty it was for her tummy. She could have offered me lobster Cantonese, and I would've turned it down in an autopsy room. After her third munch, the thought gently crossed my mind that she might be an adolescent ghoul. She had the chalk-white face for it, framed by dark brown hair, which hung straight down like dried No. 10 vermicelli. But she did have a nice sort of smile every once in a while. And a benevolent shape too. Not too fat, not too slim. Best of all was a commendable frontal insulation for the respiratory cage.*

"I didn't expect that quack to stick a knife right in the guy's throat."

"Just a trach. You'll get used to it."

"A *trach*?"

"Like in *trach*eotomy. Sometimes they have to cut into the windpipe. It's routine."

"Oh."

"A lot of people pass out the first time they see something like that. You shouldn't feel too mortified."

"I don't feel too mortified."

"Some guys might."

"I don't!"

"All right."

She took another bite of her broccoli sandwich, and our eyes met. I could tell we both knew I felt too mortified. In fact, I was so embarrassed I felt like running out of the goddamn place and finding a job at the city dump or even as a local Roto-Rooter. I mean I felt debilitated. But then I told myself what the hell.

"I hated school too, you know," she remarked, as though it were some type of conversational peace offering.

"You don't say."

---

* She had some pair of peaches.

"The one I went to had a sixteen-foot fence around it," she continued. "I think they used to cook ant shit in the cafeteria." She wiped a crumb of broccoli from her lips. "And the teachers! My home-economics teacher weighed three hundred and twenty pounds. My guidance teacher was divorced."*

"No kidding."

"And my gym teacher was a lesbian. Are you a flesh-eater?"

I sat up on the edge of the cot. She stuck her finger in the center of her brow and moved it horizontally to the left, then the right, to get her hair out of her eyes. It was like the action of a mechanical curtain rod.

"Meat," she clarified. "Do you eat meat?"

"Of course I eat meat."

"I don't."

"Why not?"

"Because I'm not a killer, that's why."

She had a strange look in her eyes, which now were about the size of copper-alloy quarters. "You must be mildly crazy," I said. I was just joking, but I could tell from the way her eyes flared that I had said the wrong thing.

"*I'm* crazy? You're the pathological flesh-eater who passes out at the sight of blood. That's a twisted, inconsistent, mildly crazy mind, if you ask me." She was breathing quite excitedly. "Could you kill a cow? Answer me that!"

"If I were hungry."

"Even if you'd raised it yourself? Could you kill it then?"

"Sure."

She leaned back against the cabinets and gritted her teeth before her next attack.

---

* The guidance teacher at my old school called me down once and asked what career I was going to undertake, and I told her undertaking. She never called me down again.

10

"If you like meat so much, why don't you eat it raw? You don't eat it raw, I'll bet."

"Of course I don't eat it raw."*

"You bet you don't!" Her voice was unbearably shrill. "You fry it, broil it, marinate it, bake it, pickle it, sauté it—you do anything to disguise the fact that it's flesh. Meats are poisons!" Her hair had flown to the center of her face, and she put her finger through the curtain-rod gesture again.

"Who says?"

"I do. I know because I'm *in tune* with my body."

I laughed out loud, and for a second I thought she was going to rush over and punch me.

She leaned forward, shaking her shoulders. "Each kind of meat poisons in a different way. If you were *in tune* with your body, you'd recognize the symptoms. If someone put so much as a speck of beef or pork in this sandwich, I'd know about it. And I'd know which meat it was from the way my body reacted!"

She took another bite, and a piece of broccoli fell. With one kick, she sent it flying across the room. That made my mind go through one of those phantasmagoric transitions it always does. I saw the piece of broccoli land near a long marble-slab table that looked something like a blood-sacrifice block, and I pictured this juicy autopsy going on—some doctor fingering an enlarged liver, like a football, when he realizes his foot is standing on something, and he looks down and sees this old piece of broccoli. Then I imagined myself being the one getting autopsied, and that brought me back to the main reason I had decided to work at a hospital. Sex.

"My name's Dewey," I said with a big smile. "What's yours?"

She looked at me for a moment as though I had become delirious.

---

* I was drunk at a picnic once in Clove Lakes Park and ate a raw hamburger, but I puked it up.

"Yvette," she finally replied.

"I beg your pardon?"

"*Yvette.*" She sounded p.o.'ed.

"That's a groovy name." I sensed my voice got a little hollow on the last remark. It was the grossest name I'd ever heard.

"You work in the inhalation department too?" I looked intensely into her eyes. I call it the old gorilla whammy because that's the way they come on when they want romance.*

"I take care of the machines," she said. "Like the Byrds. We have three Byrds."

"You're beautiful enough to be a model, you know?"

"Oh, *yeah.*"

I think she was beginning to get suspicious. "How old are you? Seventeen?"

"Eighteen," she answered. "How old are you? Twelve?"

"I might surprise you," I said, giving a little wink.

She glared, and you could just tell her larynx muscles were fighting to keep her voice under control.

"Now that you've recovered from your fainting spell, I'm sure you'll excuse me."

She started for the door, and I tried to think quickly of something clever and amusing to say. I really just wanted to know her better because she really was a little pretty, in an occult sort of way.

"Is it true what I heard?" I rattled off, tacking a ho-ho-ho-it's-joke-time laugh on the end.

She stopped and looked at me.

"Is *what* true?"

"What they say about nurses, candy-stripers, and nurse's aides."

"What do they say?"

---

* The male gorilla just gets up and walks over to the female of his choice, who's usually reclining on the veldt. He looks into her eyes, surveys her full, hairy chassis, and then jumps on her.

The turbulence on her face made me wish I had never started. "Nurses love curses, stripers want snipers, and aides like a raid?"

She gave me a long dirty look.

"Did anyone ever tell you that you're raunchy?"

The way she said it made me feel ashamed. I knew what I'd said was dumb, but somehow I couldn't stop it from coming out. "I'm sorry," I said, trying to make it sound sincere. Then I added, "I just wanted to be friendly," and that sounded puerile. "I really want to get to know you," I offered, sinking deeper at every word. "I was very interested in what you said before. About meat. You really think it's poisonous, eh?"

She opened the door.

"I was fascinated!" I practically yelled, trying to stop her from going.

"You *were?*" she asked, halting and allowing a crooked smile to creep across her face.

"Can you actually tell if someone slips you a bit of beef or pork?" I asked, with a look of bovine innocence.

"Uh-huh."

"How? I'm really interested. I really am." I gave her another gorilla whammy.

"You really want to know?"

"Yes, I do."

"Well," she started, slowly, carefully, "beef makes my stomach churn—"

"Is that so?"

"—and pork makes me *fart.*"

She slammed the door and was gone.

Chapter 3

After the first week I got into the routine of the department,* and it didn't excruciatingly impress me. Donaldson shadowed me most of the time, anxious for a mistake so he could tell me I was wrong, in a sickeningly constructive way. For example, once I was trying to screw a connection on an oxygen tank, and he said, "That's very good, Dewey, *except* that the threads tighten counterclockwise." Also, I learned he had a penchant for imparting unsolicited autobiographical details. That's how I found out he was married to a corpulent lady called Geraldine, who looked like a female Easter egg, and the two of them lived in a semi-detached garden apartment with an unclipped schnauzer named Snooky. He had a photograph of each of them on his desk, and the one of Snooky was twice as big as the one of Geraldine.

The only things new I found out about Yvette were that her last name was Goethals and that she was stealing toilet paper. The latter tawdry bit of data was unearthed because she and I were working the same shift—which was from eight in the morning to four in the afternoon—and I just happened to open the sup-

---

* Chaos.

14

ply closet next to the inhalation-therapy office, where I found her holding three rolls. Ordinarily I wouldn't have thought anything about her getting toilet paper out of the supply closet, but her neck flew into a minor spasm when I opened the door.

"Everything going all right?" she asked in an especially high falsetto.

"Just fine," I said.

She pretended to be rearranging the rolls on the shelf, but there was a worn orange-paisley Bloomingdale's shopping bag at her feet, and I had seen that in her office locker. Besides, she hadn't said a word to me since that first day when, succinctly, she informed me how her body was so melodiously in tune with vegetables but so discordant with pork. I just smiled as though I didn't know what was going on and left her in the closet. Some people embezzle millions of dollars; some rob priceless jewels. If Yvette Goethals' idea of grand larceny was three rolls of toilet paper that had the consistency of sandpaper, that was her problem. Besides, I had thought over the whole matter of what approach would be best to achieve physical familiarity with her and decided to give her the hard-to-get treatment, sadist that I am.

Donaldson had placed me in charge of the oxygen on the fourth floor, where my job was to wear a seedy white cotton jacket, which made me look like I was incessantly going to an underprivileged prom. Also, I replaced the tanks when they got close to empty and had to make sure the right number of liters per minute were flowing because not all the patients were getting the same amount. If a guy was getting one or two LPM, it meant he wasn't so bad off. If he needed five LPM, I knew he'd be gasping like a grounded catfish, and it probably wouldn't be long before they'd carry him out in a canvas bag.*

Another guy I saw in the halls was a jerk named

---

* The morgue was in the basement, next to the cafeteria.

George, who was the cleaning man for the third, fourth, and fifth floors. George was a muscular-looking guy about twenty-five, with such lightly pigmented eyes it looked like they were rolled up in his head if the light hit the wrong way. Worst of all, he was retarded and a talker. In the first five minutes I met him, he managed to describe in technicolor vignettes how he had once worked as a gym instructor at an insane asylum, was dishonorably discharged from the army for imitating nervous spasms, regretted having had his right arm tattooed with a condor clutching a scroll with MOTHER written on it, hated schnauzers, and was convinced both Yvette Goethals and Helen de Los Angeles,* who was the biweekly occupational therapist, could be had. Also, I had to come in contact with—pardon the expression—the head nurse, Miss Blotz. She was tall and thin, with glasses, and looked like a matron in charge of the kiddie section of a movie house featuring twenty cartoons and a dull flick, and the dull flick was now on. The fourth-floor day shift also boasted a handful of assorted doctor-desperate nurses.

The patients were equally obtuse. I'd be sauntering down to the water fountain and hear the whirl of wheelchair wheels and some patient would be squawking *"Doctor, doctor!"*

"I'm not a doctor," I'd say.

They'd look at me as though I were speaking North Afghanistan pig latin.

"I think I have a peptic ulcer, doctor."

There was just no telling some of them I wasn't a doctor. I suppose their mistake was understandable though, because I did handle myself in an impressively professional manner. Sometimes I'd be out in the hall, and three or four wheelchairs would come heading for me at the same time. They'd look like Dodgem

---

* Helen de Los Angeles made all the patients weave pot holders. I think she got her B.S. in pot-holding.

cars. A lady with a big wart on her forehead asked me four times a day when she was going to be discharged. The fat patients were always asking how many minutes before lunch would be served—even *after* lunch. And the two ladies in room 409—one was a dwarf—busted my chops* about regulating the oxygen. I'd show them the meter was registering two LPM, and they'd swear it was three LPM.

"We don't need three LPM!"

"Young man, are you sure it's two LPM?"

At the start of my second week I was told there was a new lady in room 400 and to rig an oxygen setup for her. An orderly had set up her nose tube since he'd had her down on the third floor for a while. Actually she had been on the third for sixteen years I found out later—had come in when there was still a lot of TB around and everybody thought she had one foot in the grave and one on a Vaselined flounder. But they tried some new drug on her, and she didn't die. She didn't get much better either, but she had managed without oxygen for most of the time. Anyway, that's what the head nurse said. Now they had moved her up to the fourth so she'd be closer to the inhalation-therapy department. I guess I should have known then the prognosis was going to be sort of horrible.

"You awake?" I asked, knocking on the half-open door. I know I was polite by most standards because George with his mop used to just walk in on the patients. He didn't even care if it was a convalescent nun getting an enema. He'd barge right in.

"Yes," came this tiny voice.

I opened the door farther and rolled a large gas cylinder along on its bottom edge.

"Got to deliver this."

---

* Last year I used that expression a lot because my mother didn't like it. Every day when I'd come home, she'd say "How was school?" and I'd say it busted my chops.

"I know."

She was sitting up. Her bed had been cranked as high as it would go, and a huge pillow was behind her head. She looked about eighty years old, and her skinny arms hung limp, like the wings of some scrawny baby bird. Her skin was wrinkled, and the tendons of her neck jutted out like flying buttresses supporting her head, and her hair had been carefully woven into two braids which spiraled on top of her head like an old coil of rope. Even her eyes were sunken, and you could see the shape of her skull. Yet somehow she wasn't ugly. She had a weird little yellow bow in her hair that made her almost cute. Actually, if someone ever told me I'd meet a wrinkled eighty-year-old sunken skull that looked cute, I'd tell them they were crazy. But she was.*

"My sugar bottle is empty," she moaned.

"Is that so?"

I swung the tank into place and started hooking up the meter and valve.

"Would you please fill it for me?"

"You'll have to ask the nurse."

"You don't understand," she said impatiently, "The bottle—"

"What bottle?"

"The one *there!*"

She pointed to a glass vial hanging just outside her window. It had a small piece of red cloth hanging from its neck, and it flapped in the wind.

"George attached it for me this morning when I was moved, but I didn't have the sugar water mixed yet."

She lifted a bony hand out toward the bed table which arched in front of her and indicated an old pickle jar filled with a cloudy liquid.

---

* I noticed a silver cup with a hinged top, sitting on her bed stand. I didn't know what it was until she cleared her throat and spit into it.

"Just a minute." I adjusted the oxygen flow to three liters, as indicated on her chart. The rubber tubing tangled for a second, but I finally straightened it out and slipped the noseband in place.

"Comfortable?"

She smiled and then let her eyes fall insistently on the pickle bottle. I grunted, unscrewed the top of the jar, and reached through the open window to fill the vial.

"What's it for?"

"Hummingbirds," she said softly.

"They like sugar water?"

"Yes," she said. "The red cloth attracts them."

"You don't say."

I looked straight into her pupils for the first time. I think she sensed I resisted smiling back and deliberately kept my voice slightly chilled. I'd learned I had to do that with the patients, or they'd boss me around until I dropped: "Fix my pillow; I need fresh water; I can't sleep; that dwarf is playing her radio too loud; pull the shades; I think my wart is growing; give me something for my peptic ulcer; get me a blanket; make a telephone call for me; rub my back; rub my behind." They'd grind you into the floor if you let them.

"I wrote a poem about hummingbirds," she said.*

"I've got to be going."

"I'll read it for you."

Her hands began to shake as she lifted them toward the bed stand. Finally she was clutching a piece of paper and holding it close to her face.

"It's not *all* about hummingbirds," she said.

"Is that so?"

"It's called 'Let's Go Back.'"

"Ma 'am, I've got work to—"

"Irene."

---

* She cleared her throat again and dropped a clam into her cuspidor.

"I beg your pardon?"

"Call me Irene. Everybody calls me Irene."

"I've got to—"

"'Let's Go Back'!" she said loudly, as if her bed stand had suddenly become a lectern.

Let's go back to the summer garden;
Let's leave this cold September.
How we loved to swing in the old cherry tree;
Hummingbirds buzzing as we laughed with glee.
That summer garden, can't you remember?
Oh, let's go back. Do. let's go back.

I looked at her for ten and a half seconds and got rigor mortis of the tongue. I hate any kind of poetry, but this was the world's worst.*

"It's beautiful," I said.

"Shall I read it again?"

"No, thank you. It was good. It really was." My left cheek began to twitch. It does that every time I'm forced to tell a lie. "I have to be going."

"I suppose you do," she said sadly. Then suddenly the sparkle returned to her eyes, and I felt as though we both knew everything the other was thinking.

"Would you mail it for me?" she asked.

"I've got to go." I tried to make my voice sound angry and started for the door.

"Please. I have it ready."

I stopped at the door and looked at her. I still couldn't get over the weird little yellow bow in her hair. As I walked slowly back to the side of the bed, she folded the paper and stuck it into an envelope. Watching her tongue run along the flap, I was won-

---

* The only poem I thought had a truly ethereal quality was:
ROSES ARE RED
VIOLETS ARE BLUE
I JUST KILLED A WOMBAT
'CAUSE IT LOOKED LIKE YOU.

dering how many million itsy-bitsy bacilli she was smearing on it.

"*The New York Times*," she said. "That's where I'm submitting this one."

"Oh?"

She went to hand me the envelope, but her arm was shaking so badly a shoe box got knocked off the bed stand. I reached out to catch it, but the lid came off, and a whole batch of envelopes scattered on the floor.

"I'm sorry," she said.

I stopped and started picking them up. I noticed they were addressed to Miss Irene Schwartzkopf* and the return addresses were ones like the *Kenyon Review*, Fairleigh Dickinson *Review, Poetry Digest, New Yorker* . . .

I put everything back on the bed stand.

"I'll straighten it," she said quickly. I could tell she was embarrassed about my seeing all the envelopes. "They're rejection slips," she said softly.

I looked at her and nodded. She handed me the new poem in its envelope.

"If you come early some morning, you may see one," she said.

"What?"

"A hummingbird." She smiled.

I had to smile back.

"They're very delicate, you know," she added. "Very delicate indeed."

---

* German for *blackhead*.

Chapter 4

In addition to toilet paper, Yvette Goethals was stealing paper towels, bandages, Mercurochrome, soap, facecloths, sheets, feminine-hygiene apparatus, pillowcases, pillows, first-aid pamphlets, nurses' handbooks, isopropyl alcohol, Kleenex tissues, antifungus lubricating lotions, and anything else she could get her hands on. I knew that because I checked her worn orange-paisley Bloomingdale's bag whenever I saw it in her locker. She brought it in empty about every third day, and by late afternoon it looked like a Westchester Red Cross Christmas stocking. She usually waited until it was time to leave before she picked up the empty bag and headed for one of the storage closets.

"Day's almost over," I said one afternoon when she arrived at the office. She had that special cherubic look on her face that told me it was carpetbagging time.

"Donaldson on his coffee break?" she asked, heading for the locker.

"Yep!"

I could hear her expel a puff of approval.

"Had a rough day?"

"Sort of."

She turned to face me, keeping the bag partially hidden behind the bottom of her uniform. She noticed my eyes fixed on it with visions of how it would only be a matter of minutes before she'd have it brimming.

"That man in room four twenty-three died, you know?" she remarked. It was the longest sentence she'd tossed to me since our brouhaha in the autopsy room. But she didn't fool me. She said it to get my attention away from the bag.

"What guy?" I inquired, trying to get my eyes as wide and innocent as hers.

"The one you *fainted* over."

"Tough."

I absolutely refused to take my eyes off the bag. She gave me a puerile smile and tried to achieve insignificance as she exited, but when she was out, I hurried to the door to see what gauze cornucopia she was raiding that afternoon. I watched her walk down the hall as casually as if she was out to pick gooseberries. Then she slipped into the autopsy room.

I counted to twenty-three slowly, then followed her. When I reached the door, I heard the whirl of a wheelchair's wheels and the woman with the wart* in the middle of her forehead came rolling out of her room across the way.

"I'm going to the bathroom, doctor," she said. She grinned at me like a mobile hyena, then suddenly accelerated stock-carishly toward the women's john. When the hall was empty, I slipped quietly into the corpse chamber.

A partition of translucent plastic just inside the door hid me for the moment. I figured out they had to put some kind of screen up or a body in process of being cut up could be seen from the hall if somebody

---

* Miss Perkivitch, a teacher in my old school, used to have a big wart on her neck, and in the spring she'd wear low-cut dresses and paste sequins on it so it looked like a diamond brooch. That's what I heard. She wore a wig too.

opened the door. I stood perfectly still, listening. When I heard the sound of savage rummaging, I knew Yvette hadn't heard me. I gave her another few seconds before peeking around the screen. There was good old Yvette, stuffing various bedding and bandaging spoils into the shopping bag.

"Bastard," I heard her say out loud. I thought she was talking to me, but then I realized she was simply disappointed in what the autopsy room had to offer in the way of five-finger discount.

Forsaking the lower regions of one cabinet, she pushed a metal stool into place, climbed up on it, and started humming contentedly. She yanked a metal tray closer to the edge of the shelf, and the humming became so joyful I thought she had unearthed a bevy of Bulova watches. It turned out to be a bunch of scissors of varying sizes. She took one large pair of shears and bulls-eyed them into the shopping bag below. It looked like she was going to let a tiny delicate pair of scissors fly, but then opened a button on the top of her uniform and tucked them down her front. I figured now was as good a time as any to walk out from behind the screen.

"Hi!" I yelled.

She let out a noise that sounded like *aaaaaarrrrr-ghhhhhh* and almost fell off the stool.

"What's ya doin'?" I asked colloquially.

"J . . . j . . . just straightening up."

"That's nice," I said, helping her down. "Time to go home, and here you are tidying up a room you don't even work in."

I sat on the stool and gave her a big friendly smile. "You looked as if you were after something special."

"No."

"It looked that way."

She took a deep breath, and I could tell she was trying to think of a lie.

"In a way I *was* looking for something. One of the Byrd-machine attachments was missing, and I thought it might have found its way in here. Autopsy auto-claves anything they get their hands on, you know."

She let out a nervous laugh, and I tried to keep my eyes focused right into hers. She bent over quickly and covered the shears in the shopping bag with a fold of sheet. When she straightened up, my eyes almost popped out of their sockets because the pair of small scissors she had tucked down her front had wiggled upward so the cutting edges were peeking out of the top of her bra like the head of a stainless-steel asp.* She automatically closed the open button, but you could still see the shape of the scissors. We smiled at each other.

"I have to be going," she said. She picked up her bag and started off. As she pulled open the door, I was at her heels. She turned quickly and looked ninety-eight percent disconcerted that I was still right next to her.

"Bye now," she said, her voice climbing in v.p.s.

"Bye," I said, still on her heels.

"See you tomorrow."

"Yep."

She couldn't understand how she kept saying good-bye to me but I was still next to her. And I could tell the pair of scissors tucked in her front was bothering her.

"Aren't you going back to the office?" I asked.

"No."

"Oh."

I hurried along at her side. *"I guess you have everything,"* I couldn't help adding.

"Well, so long now." She halted to see if I would continue down the hall. "I'm stopping in the ladies' room a moment."

"Oh, yeah?" I said, halting. "Miss Blotz just went in."

---

* By this time I began to realize that Yvette Goethals was a very modern girl. You might say she was abreast of the times.

"Miss Blotz?"

I knew that would get her. "Didn't you notice her?"

Suddenly she looked angry. "Well, what are *you* waiting for?"

I smiled. "When Miss Blotz comes out, I think she should know about all the extra work you do around here. You ought to get credit for this sort of thing. Get what you deserve."

"No," she said. "You don't mention me to anybody, do you understand?" She looked as if she was ready to give me the kiss of death. "Just mind your own business." She darted into a stairwell.

"Aren't you going to the john?" I called after her. I gave her enough time to get down one flight, and then I thumped down the stairs myself. I didn't want her to have a second to retrieve the scissors. By the time I got to the main floor exit, she had already cut through the hedges to the oval drive in front of the regular hospital entrance. She was moving very fast along the curving sidewalk.

I waited until she was off the hospital grounds before I caught up to her.

"Hi!" I said again.

She stopped dead in her tracks, and this time her eyes were inflamed.

"What the hell kind of a crazy pisser are you?" she growled. I had no idea her voice could get so raspy.

"A *what*?" I inquired.

I thought she was making an obscene gesture, but she diverted her finger to the center of her brow for the parting of the hairs. She started off again.

I walked along with her, even though she'd started making terrible sounds under her breath.

"I just wanted to be friends," I advised.

"Pick on somebody else."

"Don't you want me to walk you home?"

"No!"

"They say if any two people are exposed to each other long enough, they begin to like each other."

26

She fumed. "I don't want you exposed to me."

I began whistling. Then my left cheek began to twitch.

"I'm sorry for coming on so strong last week."

"*Ummmm.*"

"I am."

I noticed a lessening of the shade of scarlet in her left eye, so I let her digest the apology as we crossed a busy intersection. A car headed for us, and I gave her arm an assist. She shook it loose like a muskrat freeing its leg from a trap.

"Like me to carry the shopping bag?"

She didn't answer.

"It's looks so *heavy.*"

She still didn't answer.

"Maybe you'd like to stop for a brew?"

"Why *me?*" she finally said, with a snort of disgust.

"Are you sure you wouldn't like a nice cool brew?"

"No!" She shook her head. "Invite George out. He'd go. Get him a couple of beers and tattoo his other arm. Better yet, tattoo his ass."

I burst into laughter so loud some lady was startled and bumped her baby carriage into a hydrant. I kept laughing extra long because I could tell it was placating Yvette.

"Don't you have *friends?*" she asked, looking at me for a moment, then turning her sights straight ahead again. She was plodding now from the weight of the shopping bag.

"I had one good friend—Joey Tesserone.* He moved to Santa Monica, California. I hitchhiked out, but it wasn't the same. His family came into a little money, and now for brunch they serve soufflés and hot cross buns on the lawn. The worst part about it

---

* Joey Tesserone had a screw loose. He tried smoking bananas once, almost died from poison sumac, and whenever we got loaded, he insisted on throwing moons at the police station.

27

was he said he *likes* hot cross buns and soufflés on the lawn."

"Don't you have a girl friend?"

"I did."

"What'd you do with her?"

"We hung out together a lot. Seven months in our freshman year, but she won't talk to me anymore."

"Why not?"

"She was incinerated in South Carolina. A plane crash."*

"That's too bad."

"It is."

"There must be somebody who can stand you that's still surviving."

"Most of my good friends went to college this fall. I saw a couple of them on weekends in October, but they were all talking about *The Myth of Sisyphus*, and I didn't know what *The Myth of Sisyphus* was. I thought it was a disease." I let my voice reach a new plaintive low.

"Ummmmmm."

"I'll bet *you* were popular in school," I said.

"Crap."

"Really? I'm surprised."

"My school was crammed with pimple-faced kids wearing love medallions, running around calling fat kids wearing love medallions *fat*, and fat kids wearing love medallions, running around calling pimple-faced kids wearing love medallions *pimple-faced*."

"What?"

"Forget it," she said. Then suddenly she seemed possessed. "Hypocrisy! That's what I'm talking about. The kids in my school were the biggest collection of prejudiced, rotten, spiteful, hateful, lousy, corrupt,

---

* Vivian Johnson was her name, and she was a nice girl even though she wasn't smart. When she made up a shopping list, it looked like this: 1 bag marchmellows, 1 Ivrey soap, 1 krakojacks, 1 package ostrettes and ass. cookies, 1 fig nooten, 1 lofe raison bred, and 1 jar jerken pickles.

vile, love-medallion-wearing cannibals I ever saw. And frankly you give me the same impression."

I couldn't speak for a whole minute. Nobody had ever previously referred to me as a prejudiced, rotten, spiteful, hateful, lousy, corrupt, vile, love-medallion-wearing cannibal before. I had a good mind to be insulted and let her go on by herself. But then I said what the hell.

"Do you mind my walking you home?"

"You're *not* walking me home."

"Parents strict?"

"No."

"Then why not?"

"Because."

"Because why?"

"I don't live with my parents."

"So why can't I walk you home?"

"That's my business."

"Why don't you live with them?"

"Because they're bastards. My mother's a dumb one. My father's a mean one."

"Did you run away?"

"Uh-huh."

"They don't know where you are?"

"I ran away five months ago. They had the cops after me at first, but when I finally called them and told them I found them mentally disgusting, they left me alone. Danny ran away too. He's my brother. Sixteen. I think he's a fag."

"That's too bad."

"Is it?"

I coughed.

"Why is your mother a dumb bastard?"

"Don't call her that. It's all right for me, but not you." She transferred the shopping bag from one hand to the other. I caught another glimpse of the stainless-steel asp.*

---

* I heard that in nudist colonies nobody looks below the neck.

"She keeps getting pregnant," she continued. "That's her main problem. I have four brothers and three sisters. My sister Regina got married last Sunday. I didn't go. She just married to get out of the house."

The lights changed against us at the corner of Clove Road and Forest Avenue. She stopped and set the shopping bag down.

"This is as far as you're going," she said.

"I'll walk you home."

"Nope."

I tensed my eyes, trying to squeeze a bit of moisture into them so she'd think I was emotionally distraught. "Do I really give you the impression I'm a *cannibal?* I mean, we've got a lot of things in common. We're both dropouts and . . ."

Her eyes turned on me like a pair of battleship guns. I knew I'd said the wrong thing again.

"Look, Dewey-Smewey whateverthefuckyourname-is. Don't put me in the same class with you."

"I actually give that much of a puerile impression?"

"I'll tell you what kind of an impression you give. Do you really want to know?"

"Yes, I do."

"You come off like a lazy spoiled punk whose Momsy and Popsy think they're committing some type of middle-class progressiveness by letting you drop out of school because you bellyached too much about cracking a book. That's not my bag. And, *physically*, do you want to know what you remind me of physically?"

I gulped.

"Yes. Yes, I would."

"Physically, with that shock of mouse-brown hair, that haughty stupid prance as soon as you put on your white lab jacket, like it's let's-play-Doctorville, and those rodent eyes that smell out every mirror to see if you look as marvelous as you think you do—including that chin you puff out like a turtle—anyway, the whole outside makes you look like a leering virgin.

And mentally, or metaphysically, I don't think you give a bird turd about politics, social problems, racism, religion, law enforcement, world famine, or anything. In short, I think you're just one more of our sick society's ridiculous, dangerous wastes. That's what I think."

The light changed, and she started to cross. Several people started from the other side, and I think if they hadn't been there, I would have gone after her and phantasmagorically socked her. I never hit a girl in my life, but if you asked me, at that moment Yvette Goethals needed a good kick in the rear.

"At least I'm not a crook!" I yelled from my corner. "I don't go around stealing things from a public hospital!"

The other people on the street were staring by the time she got to the other side.

"Hey, everybody!" I belted out. "She's got that shopping bag loaded with stuff she stole from your public hospital! You paid for them with your taxes, and she's stealing them!"

She spun around and glared at me.

"*He's a maniac!*" she screamed.

"Oh, yeah?" I bellowed. "All anybody has to do is look at your chest, and they'll see a pair of scissors tucked in your bra. Honest people don't go around with scissors tucked in their bras."

She looked like a pigmy volcano as she put her hand to her chest. She backed up a few steps as several passersby stopped and looked. Finally, she turned and started to run.

"Is that what they mean by *cleavage?*" I bellowed, loud enough to make sure she heard it. In fact, I made sure everyone on the next block heard that one.

Chapter 5

That Friday night I stayed home and watched an old flick on television—about two kids who fall in love and the authorities had to put *him* away in the nut house. Saturday night I went out and got loaded at this place in South Beach that looks like an authentic English pub. They call it The Authentic English Pub. It's rather celebrated among my peers because they serve you if you show the least bit of pubescence. One kid I know is fourteen, and he goes in with a plastic moustache, and they set him up. The police lay off the place, I guess, because the owner is a veteran from World War II. He's also paraplegic.

I had an intensely lousy time because I met one girl who had nice legs. Her face wasn't bad either. The problem was she had one hair growing out of her nose. Also she was torso-less. It looked like her shoulders were attached right to her hips, and when I danced with her, I got nonplussed trying to figure out what she did with her waist. Another strike against her was she was drinking Bloody Marys—and drinking them fast.*

---

* To be fair, I must admit she had a lot of personality. Also, she wore a very seductive perfume which I think was an exclusive Paris brand called Eau De Halitosis.

I suppose the real *plotz* was that every time I went to the john and looked in the mirror, I heard Yvette Goethals calling me a leering virgin. And the drunker I got, the more furious I was about what she'd said concerning my middle-class Momsy and Popsy. No matter what she thought, my parents did not cripple me emotionally, transfigure my id, or use my libido for a trampoline. My folks happen to be plain, nice, detached, insignificant people, and nobody has the right to pin any rap on them. With names like Theodore and Antoinette, they've had it hard enough in life. My mother is a gracious librarian, whose only blemish is a little Dewey Decimal of the brain. And my father is a smog-control engineer, which means he gets twenty thousand bucks a year for running up on roofs and jamming a cork in a bottle. And even though my name is Dewey, my mother swears she didn't name me after you-know-what, although I personally think she was a little influenced by 574.09T. The important thing is they leave me alone and let me live my own life. So I'm keeping my sweet, lovely, gentle, and kind mother and father out of this. Besides, they'd sue.

Sunday, I went out to a movie by myself. It was a horror flick, advertised not to be an exploitation film because the explicit nude scenes were required in order to understand the multiple ax murders. After that, I came home and sat in my room, smoking. Cigarettes. That's when I knew something unusual was going on inside of me. I don't usually smoke in my room. I used to do the whole bit last year—strap on the stereo earphones and puff down to the filters. Now, I kept thinking of Yvette Goethals, and there were two feelings going on inside at the same time. One minute I felt warm and titillated, contemplating her body. Next I'd hear her enunciating "leering cannibalistic virgin," and I'd feel asthmatic. That night I had a dream.

I'm swimming in the ocean off Sandy Hook, without

any clothes on, when a commercial fishing vessel comes sailing along and anchors nearby to catch eels. There's a whole crowd of Mongolian-looking people lined along the railings, and they're busy sticking squid and blood-oozing sandworms onto hooks and waving them at me. I smile back, but I'm really worried about them seeing that I don't have any clothes on. That's when I start drowning. I scream for help, and all the Mongolian weirdos start casting their squid and blood-oozing sandwormed hooks at me, and a couple of the barbs slice into my chest. I am suddenly in dire pain. Even though I'm drowning, I pull the fish hooks out and keep calling for help; then I spy Yvette Goethals in a transparent bikini, near the bow of the ship, and she throws a rope to me. I grab it and she guides me to the side, and even though I'm nude, I don't mind coming out of the water and standing next to her. About then I think some of the weirdos started taking Polaroid shots.

That's when I woke up.

On Monday I bought a dozen roses at Richmond Florist and made sure I got to work fifteen minutes early. I had them in a brown paper bag just in case someone from the night shift was around, but it augured well because the office was empty. I stuck the bouquet in Yvette's locker. No card. No note. Then I went to the employee's john because I didn't want to be around when she arrived. I had a smoke and reread some of the better graffiti.* A new one was rather puerile: PLEASE DO NOT THROW BUTTS IN THE URINALS. IT MAKES THEM SOGGY AND HARD TO LIGHT. About 8:02 I went back to the office.

"Good morning," Donaldson said, looking up from

---

* What are you looking up here for? You're dripping on your shoe! Gargantua was queer. Miss Blotz sucks. God is alive—it's you that's dead. Chinese basket job—TQ 9-1212—after 6 P.M.

his desk. He had a light-green jacket on, making him look like a pistachio Easter egg.

"Hello," I said.

Yvette was standing at the rear of the office with her back to me. She half turned, then went back to rinsing a machine attachment that was shaped like a duck's foot. Glancing at her locker, I saw the roses had been placed in a bottle of water, and that made my ego feel quasi-resurrected.

"Snooky took third," Donaldson commented.

"I beg your pardon?"

"At the Travis Dog Show. My wife and I entered Snooky on Sunday."

"I'm sorry."

"Sorry about what?"

"That Snooky only got third place."

"He's lucky he got that."

He grunted and started going through some papers. I went to my locker and donned my ghetto prom jacket. As I slipped it on, I could hear Yvette's voice still resounding on my eardrum: *Do you want to know what I think of you physically? Do you?*" I walked across the room with as little of a haughty prance as possible. She appeared to be engrossed in drying the attachment she was holding. I paused for a moment.

"I'll start checking tanks," I said.

"I think it was the way my wife handled him," Donaldson lamented. "Snooky's performance was fine. It was Geraldine who tripped in front of the judges."

The next morning I decided to put a Fanny Farmer nut-candy log in Yvette's locker. This time I left a little card that simply said "Hello." When I came up from having a smoke, Yvette wasn't in the office, but I could tell she'd punched in because her worn orange-paisley Bloomingdale's shopping bag was in her locker and inside it was the Fanny Farmer nut-candy log. About ten minutes later I was walking down the hall when Yvette came heading toward me. That situation

35

had happened once on Monday, but she turned off into the room containing the two ladies—where one of them is a dwarf. I know she did it so we didn't have to come face to face, because she had once remarked that the dwarf* made her skin creep. But this time she kept coming straight at me.

She spoke. "Mr. Donaldson asked me to tell you there's an Ox change in room four hundred." She spun on her heel and started away.

"Thank you," I said.

That mealy-mouthed confrontation had produced such palpitations in my pancreas that I walked into room 400 in a daze. There was Irene, cranked up, sitting with her tiny head against the huge pillow, the speck of a bow neatly tied in the coil of rope on her head.

"Good morning," I said.

She smiled, but I could see she wasn't quite as perky as she'd been the week before.

"I'm such a bother," she said.

"No, you're not."

"I don't *need* four liters per minute."

I checked the chart at the bottom of the bed and saw the doctor's orders.

"You just do what the doctor says," I told her. I adjusted the meter and could see the increase let her breathe easier. It was obvious she knew the difference too.

"I don't need it."

"Did you have any hummingbirds this morning?"

"Three."

"No kidding?"

"Two at six thirty-seven and the other one was around eight." She cleared her throat and leaned for-

---

* The dwarf was really a very kind lady who used to hand out a lot of free Clark bars. I like all dwarfs anyway, because they're the only people I know who truly look up to me.

ward to reach the sputum cup. I pretended not to notice as she pressed the handle which lifted the top. She let a clam plop right in.

"Oh, dear."

"What's the matter?"

"It's full."

"I'll empty it."

"Would you?"

"Sure."

"I could ring for one of the nurses."

"I don't mind."

I reached out to lift the thing, and she began to shake her hands at me. The oxygen tubes had slipped from her nose, and she had to set them straight before she could explain what she was excited about.

"I wrote a new poem."

I looked at the big smile on her face, then at the sputum cup.

"After I empty—"

"No, please. Then you could mail it for me, and it'd make the ten-thirty pickup." She leaned closer to the bed stand and freshened the lace collar of her bed jacket. "This is going to the London *Observer*. They're more sensitive over there."

"What happened to 'Let's Go Back'?"

"It came back this morning."

"I'm sorry. I thought it was a nice poem."

"This one," she said, taking up a piece of paper, "is called 'I Thought Of You Today.' Ready?"

"I guess so."

I thought of you today,
The lovely boy who sat next to me,
Was it History or Geometry?
We never spoke, we never shared
Our dream of Spring or secrets bared.
In silence though I hope you knew
I cared, I cared, just never dared,
But I thought of you today.

I nodded solemnly, as though I'd just received some kind of ultra-archidiocese benediction. Actually, I thought this one was so abominable I was afraid I'd have to use her cuspidor.*

"I'd better empty this."

The way she glowed I knew she was still hallucinating over her latest creation. Her eyes were cast heavenward, but regardless of the celestial stupor, she still managed to slip the poem into an addressed envelope and push it toward me. With my free hand, I tucked it into my lab coat.

I turned and started for the door, holding the sputum cup by its handle and keeping my eyes glued to the lid. If I tilted it the slightest bit, I knew the gook would come gushing down the sides. I wasn't worried about galloping bacilli because I had checked that one out with Miss Blotz, and she said tuberculosis wasn't Irene's problem anymore. "Oh, Irene's negative," Miss Blotz said. "She's negative." Now it was emphysema, and some kind of deterioration of the pleural cavity, whatever that is. I inched down the hall and was very close to a sink cabinet when there was the usual whirl of a wheelchair's wheels. I just knew I was going to spill the works. That's the way it always happens. I'm afraid something's going to happen, and something comes along that might make it happen, and it's only because I'm afraid it's going to happen that really makes it happen. Anyway, the wheelchair went by, with the lady with the wart in the middle of her forehead. It didn't even touch me, but I spilled a big slop of sputum right on the side of the hall. I managed to get the rest of it emptied into a

---

* My second most-beloved poem in the world is that old classic:
THEY ASKED ME HOW I KNEW
RACCOON SHIT WAS BLUE
I COULD NOT DENY
IN MY TERSE REPLY
ONE FELL IN MY EYE.

sink which was only a few yards farther, but I didn't savor the idea of wiping up the plop in the corridor. Besides, I had a coffee break coming up, and the Richmond Valley Hospital beverages were hard enough to engulf without having to precede them with a clam harvest.

"How ya doin', Dewey?" I heard this rough voice behind me.

"Fine."

George flashed a great big jackass smile and rubbed his arm just below the condor holding the scroll with *MOTHER* written on it, so now all you could see was *MOTH*. I continued running water into the empty sputum cup and at first didn't take particular notice of the mop and pail he was holding.

"De Los Angeles in today?" he queried.

"Yes."

"She's got me doing a pot holder."

I took a close look at him, and for a second, thought I had been transported back to the Cro-Magnon epoch.

"Did I tell you I'm reading a book on X-ray technique?"*

"No, George, you didn't."

"If I was a technician, I bet she'd go out with me, that's what I think."

"Sure, George."

"All she thinks of me now is as a *crappickerupper!*"

His last predicate got through to me. "Listen, George," I started.

"What?"

"You know the dwarf?"

"Yeah."

"Well, her mother brought her in some Chinese food this morning. We told her it was against the

---

* The last book George was reading was titled *The End of Fanny Hill's Fanny.*

rules, and she went to dump it, but accidentally spilled some over there." I pointed.

"Want me to get it?"

"Would you, George?"

He bounded off with his pail and mop, like an orangutan in a circus act. I quickly lifted the sputum cup out of the sink and wrapped it in paper towels to hide it. Then I tried to pass George as fast as possible.

"What the hell kind of food was it?" he asked.

"Wonton and lobster sauce," I said.

That afternoon I spent my break in the autopsy room. I guess I knew all along I was going to write a letter:

Dear Yvette:

I'm leaving work five minutes early today, so by the time you find this in your shopping bag I'll be gone and you can read it without anxiety. Even save it until you get home, but the important thing is that you read it. First of all I want you to know I didn't tell anybody about your pilfering passion for toilet paper and other supplies. I don't care if you steal the entire cardiovascular care unit. Maybe you're making up gift packages for orphans. I don't know. I just yelled those things out on the street because you found it incumbent upon yourself to put me down. All I can say is you can't take people on the surface. You've got to get to know them. It works two ways, you know. Just because you were shoving scissors down your brassiere didn't soil your reputation with me. You probably have a good reason why you did it, and I'm willing to wait until you feel like talking about it. I'm not saying I don't have problems. I do. But you're wrong about blaming my mother and father. It's my puerile peers you've got to blame. Yvette, I'm a lonely guy, and I really only wanted to be friends with you. I'm not desperate—don't get that idea. This weekend I went out and did a lot of things. Did you ever go to The Authentic English Pub? I met a nice girl and had a good time. So I'm not desperate. But my friends have always given me the shaft, ever since I can remember. I'm not telling you this to be pornographic, but even in the third grade my best friend, Jackie Kohild, double-crossed me. We had worked half the summer, making insectariums in my backyard.* We each dug a hole about the size of a bushel basket and caught all the different insects we could—centipedes, crickets, assorted larvae, daddy longlegs, etc., and put them in along with leaves, twigs, and rocks. Everything was fine until we started displaying our insectariums to Jeanette Matischewitz, a peer who used to love climbing the apple tree in my yard. That was OK until I found a black widow spider one afternoon, and Jeanette Matischewitz made such a big fuss over it my friend got jealous. The next morning I found somebody had defecated† in my insectarium, and I knew it was Jackie Kohild. Actually I realize now that Jackie must have always had a deep-seated problem because I read in the paper just last year that he was arrested for having noxious liquids in Wolf's Pond Park. I always got the double cross. I suppose that's why I write a letter when I want someone to really understand me. Maybe I do give the physical and metaphysical impression you say I do, but if I write something down, it tells much more about me inside. A lot of people say I have a superior vocabulary, and some think I'm being haughty when I exercise it. The only reason I like words is because I was the first one in the fifth grade who could spell Mississippi and the teacher made a big fuss over it. If my science teacher had ever made a big fuss over me, I'd probably be an astrophysicist. That's the breaks. As far as I can gather, your main complaint about me is that I don't care about the problems of the world. Well, you're wrong. I'm very much concerned about the lousy criminals that infest our government, and I can't sleep nights sometimes, thinking about race hatred and wondering if our polluted rivers and lakes will ever be reclaimed. Don't you think the fact that cops are such crooks and that people are starving to death

---

* I want to go on record as having refuted Darwin's theory of evolution in H.S. bio. As far as I'm concerned, an insect can mutate and *survive to the fittest* from now until doomsday, and it will never end up looking exactly like a special kind of twig or leaf, like some of them do. I'm for a rebirth of environmental influence on genes. I have a rabies theory too, but this footnote is too long already.
† crapped

affects me? I'm very involved. And nobody thinks more about death than I do, Yvette. Don't you realize that you and I are going to end up in a coffin soon enough? Can't we at least be friends before our time comes? If you'd only give me a chance. You're probably saying to yourself "Why me?" again. Well, I have a feeling about you. I have a feeling you're a very special individual. I have a vision that in some weird and bizarre way you and I have a destiny with each other. Could we go out Friday night? Please answer me. I'm going to send you flowers or candy every day until you do. Let's be friends, Yvette, before it's too late.

Sincerely yours,
Dewey Daniels

Chapter 6

The next morning I was sticking a dozen fuchsia gladioli into Yvette's locker when she walked in and caught me. Her face twisted into a frown, and she advanced, practically pushing me away from the locker. Without a word, she went about her business of changing into a lab coat.

"Hi," I said.

She looked at me like I was a living indiscretion, and I could see the neck muscles begin to vibrate preparatory to some sort of supersonic utterance.

"Look," she said, "you want to take me out Friday?"

I could feel extreme shock distorting my eyeballs. I blinked three times. "What?"

"Do you want to take me out Friday or don't you?"

"Yes."

"OK."

"OK?"

"That's what I said. OK."

"OK." I said. I do that sometimes when the blood rushes to my head. I OK somebody to death.

"How much were the glads?" she asked. As she leaned into the locker, her voice echoed as though in a cave.

"What?"

"The gladiolas. How much were they?"

"Three dollars."*

She straightened up, looked at herself in a mirror on the metal door, and brushed her hair out of her eyes. She began smoothing the collar of her lab jacket, as though stalling for time.

"Look, if you meant what you said in that letter—" she started.

"I did."

She looked at me via the mirror. "I mean, if you meant the part about bringing me flowers or candy every day—"

"I did."

"I just want to make it clear that I don't appreciate crap like that. You don't mind my telling you, do you?"

"Oh, no. I want us to be honest with each other."

"Would you like to know what I *would* appreciate?"

"Yes. Yes, I would."

She spit on her right forefinger and ran it over her eyebrows. "Seeds."

"*Seeds?*"

"Vegetable seeds. Beans, wheat, barley. That sort of thing. That's the kind of present I'd enjoy. I'm just saying if you ever decide to present me with any other tokens of friendship, that's what I'd really like. OK?"

She gave me a smile and started for the door. My stomach was squishing so nervously it stopped me from thinking of one other question I wanted to ask. It came to me when she was almost out.

"Yvette!"

She halted and looked at me. Her nostrils narrowed, and I was afraid I had triggered her adrenal glands.

"What?"

"Shall I pick you up?"

She ruminated a moment.

---

* Two dollars.

"I'll be on the corner of Clove Road and Forest Avenue."

"What time?"

"Nine thirty." She turned to go, then had another thought. "By the way, when I say seeds, I don't mean a little package for some kindergarten window box. Onic's hardware in Four Corners sells them by the pound, if you know what I mean."

I nodded.

"There's a hardy type of Burpee big-kernel corn I could use."

She smiled.

I smiled.

She made an infinitesimal bow, like a geisha girl forced to show respect to a Pakistani untouchable, and then went her way.

Friday, I made sure I was on the corner a half hour early. It was the first time I had gotten dressed up for a date in a long time. Not that I was wearing a tie, but I had my good dark-blue-with-a-yellow-stripe sport jacket on. I had no idea what costume she would show up in. Personally, I wouldn't have been surprised if she appeared in a fig leaf and psychedelic pasties.* I sat on the bus-stop bench for a while, smoking. Even though the streets were well lit, I was a bit uncomfortable with Clove Lakes Park right behind me. A lot of the more colorful muggings and rapes go on in there. Only a few lampposts light the walk that snakes down to the lake, and there are a lot of hiding places. The thought even crossed my mind that Yvette might have set up an ambush. Maybe she was a moll in some sadomasochistic** gang, and they were going to attack with tire irons and chains. Tie me up and tickle me with fuchsia gladioli or some-

---

* Tommy Toilet-Tongue said she once went to a party dressed as a marijuana plant and wore a sign on her behind that said "Keep Off the Grass."

** What do people see in sadomasochism? It beats me.

45

thing. I mean, I didn't really know anything about her.

At nine thirty I looked up and down the street, but no one was in sight. She might not even show, I thought. Suddenly there was a noise behind me, and I glanced into the park, only to see what I thought was a bear bounding up from the lake. This big glob of fur was heading straight for me, and I bolted up off the bench. Then I recognized Yvette Goethals' cranium protruding from the top of the mound, and I knew it was one of those artificial mouton lamb coats or something. She had it open in the front, and every once in a while a breeze would catch it, and she doubled in size. I mean, winter wasn't too far off, but I think it was a little early for a grizzly outfit. She waved a huge tote bag at me, which sent her hair into an uproar, making her faintly reminiscent of a wolf-woman.

"Hi," I said when she was on top of me, pardon the expression.

"Hi," she said.

"Nice night, eh?"

I fumbled in my jacket for my cigarettes. Then I had to fight the breeze to get one lit.

"Where are we going?" she asked.

I got a glimpse of what she was wearing under the coat. It looked like plaid culottes and a man's white shirt, with a rainbow-colored scarf tied around her waist.

"How about a movie?"

"I hate movies."

"We could have a few drinks and talk."

She sat down on the bench and pulled up her ugly orange knee socks.*

"Would you like that?" I pursued.

---

* Her gams were splendid. I knew a girl once that had twelve toes. Saw a cow in a freak show that had seven legs—also some kid that had a face like a donkey and sang "Let Me Call You Sweetheart."

"I don't know."

There was something about the way she made that last remark that gave the impression she knew precisely what she wanted to do but it was up to me to guess.

"Have you ever been to The Authentic English Pub?"

"No."

"Would you like that?"

I sat on the bench next to her, and she reached for my chest. I jerked reflexively until I realized she was putting her hand into my jacket to get a cigarette.

"They're mentholated," I said.

"I'm not going to smoke it." She put the cigarette to my lips. "Light it, please."

I used my own butt, and when I got hers going, she just sat holding it.

"I gave up smoking two months ago. Now I just enjoy holding one occasionally and watching it burn."

"Oh."

"Listen, Dewey . . ." She hesitated.

"What?"

She gave me a look, as if she was annoyed at having to restrain herself in my presence. I smiled, wanting to encourage her to say whatever was on her mind.

"Is something the matter?"

"No."

"If you've got something bugging you, just tell me. I'll understand."

She made a sound with her tongue on the roof of her mouth. "*Tuuuuucccccch.*"

"Really?" I said. I meant it as a ha-ha.

"Well, it's just that if we had gone to the movies, it would have cost you at least five dollars. Right?"

"I suppose . . . so."

"Well, I could use that five dollars."

"I don't understand."

"I'd rather have the five dollars cash."

"You want me to give you the money I would have spent if we had gone to the movies?"

"Would you?"

I started to sigh, but changed it into a cough. "If you want."

"You don't mind?"

"Why should I mind?"

I dug into my right front pants' pocket and pulled out a bunch of bills. I gave her a five like it was nothing, and she crammed it into her tote bag. We sat in silence for a full minute before she said, "We could go for a beer if you like. I mean if you had been planning on a movie *and* a few beers."

"Yes, I had," I said. I couldn't help adding, "They only sell bottle beer on Friday, and that's fifty cents a throw. If you *prefer* the cash—"

"No."

"You sure?"

"Positive."

She didn't sound all that positive.

"Then we're off to The Authentic English Pub!" I said.

"Er . . ." she sputtered.

"You don't want to go to The Authentic English Pub?" I asked.

"I like the Bridge Cafe better."

"Where's that?"

"Near the Bayonne Bridge."

"Is that the place they have all the knife fights?"

"Not every night."

"Why do you want to go there? It's dangerous."

She started to take a puff of her cigarette, stopped herself in time, and casually flicked the ash. Then she stood up, pulled the artificial mouton lamb coat snug around her, and tilted her head. "They have a good band."

"All right," I said reluctantly. "We can get the bus across the street."

"Oh, no," she blurted. Before I could stop her she

had trotted into the middle of the road and was walking backwards down Forest Avenue with her thumb sticking out.

"What're you doing?" I yelled.

"Hitching."

"Hitching?"

Her thumb flagellated the light beams of an oncoming car as I crossed the street and caught up to her.

"The bus fare wouldn't be more than fifty cents."

"Fifty cents going, fifty cents coming," she calculated. "You can give me the buck."

A car screeched to a halt.

We got in the backseat of this decrepit car, with a matching decrepit man driving and a decrepit lady sitting next to him. The old guy accelerated the car like it was a lubricated bat out of hell. Yvette and I gasped audibly, but the old lady just sat, calmly stupefied. I think she was having a mumbled conversation with either the glove compartment or the white-plastic St. Christopher statue glued to the dashboard.

"You kids go to school?" the guy asked, turning his head for a second and flashing a pair of drunken salmon-colored eyes.

"Tottenville High," Yvette said, giving me a little grin.

"No kidding? I teach at Franklin High School," the old guy said.

I could see Yvette rotating slowly to the left, to see more of the old lady's face. She was still mumbling.

"Went to Ginny's Pizzeria," the man said. "You been to Ginny's Pizzeria?"

"No."

"They've got good pizza," he said. He let out a raucous laugh. "Good beer too."

"What subject do you teach?" Yvette asked.

The guy flashed his eyes around, as though he didn't particularly like this question. He burped revoltingly and didn't respond for a full minute; then it was by changing the subject.

"We got stopped by the police," he said.

"What for?" I asked.

"Said we were speeding. Then they saw my wife." He silently mouthed the following words to us: "SHE'S AN ALCOHOLIC."

"I'm sorry," Yvette said.

"Don't be. Nobody else is." He reached his hand to his neck and straightened the ugly, loud tie he was wearing. It looked like it was made of the same material as his wife's dress, which was something like curdled corduroy.* "I told the cop I was a teacher. You know—both working for the city. That routine. Usually works. This one gave me a ticket anyway. I didn't say anything while he wrote it out, but when he gave it to me, I checked his name and looked him right in the eye. I said, "Thanks, Officer Rattray. That's a very interesting name, *Rattray*. Just in case you ever have kids attending Franklin High, I'll make sure I remember it. I want to be as nice to them as you've been to me."

"You can let us off at the light," Yvette said.

He began braking the car as though he was pushing organ pedals for a scherzo fugue.

We got a full-face view of him as we got out, including the vista of veins protruding from his swollen nose. His wife even turned at the sound of the door opening, and she looked exactly like him but with a wig on.

"I teach law and economics," the guy said.

"Thanks for the ride," I said.

Yvette slammed the door, threw her tote bag over her shoulder, and began running down the street, toward the blinking neon sign of the Bridge Cafe. You

---

* There was one nice feature about the decrepit driver—he had a very attractive hearing aid plugged into his right ear.

could hear the band already. She stopped in front and waited.

"You stay out here for five minutes," she said. "Then come in and stand behind me at the bar."

"What for?"

"Just do what I say."

The first thought that went through my mind was that she was ashamed to be seen with me.

"All right," I said.

There was a crowd of guys around the front entrance, and I watched Yvette elbow her way into them and disappear inside. There and then, I was going to clear out. I figured it's one thing, making a pass at a curvaceous kleptomaniacal co-worker whose penchant is pilfering toilet paper and wearing scissor falsies, but I had no intention of risking my life by going into some bar where everybody is just itching for a head to bash a beer bottle over. And I'd have to tell any guy that called her an abominable mouton monstrosity to shut up, which would be hard because even I thought she looked like an abominable mouton monstrosity. No siree, I wasn't going to get a knife stuck in my guts. Not in a million years.

Then I said what the hell.

Chapter 7

The smoke was so thick it looked like levitating meringue, and the band had the amps turned up high enough for me to think somebody was using a tack hammer to play "The Flight of the Bumblebee" on my inner ear. The bar was a big oval affair, with a crowd standing seven-deep around it. The guys all looked like they drove eight-axle cement trucks in the morning, dug ditches in the afternoon, and for kicks in the evening swam three miles and pressed five hundred pounds.* There was about one girl for every five guys, and most of them had bleached Marie Antoinette coiffures and looked like they had been lowered recently from birdcages on some street in Bombay where you pay for pulchritude. Either that or they'd just done eighty-three laps on an unrosined roller-derby track.

I saw Yvette at the far end of the bar, pouring the contents of a bottle of beer into a glass in front of her. At first, I thought she had actually bought it herself, but as I moved closer I saw she was batting her eyes at a muscular bull elephant sitting next to her. She

---

* There was one guy that did look puny—like the kind of person whose idea of a really good time is to sit around pointing out spiritual values in Beethoven gavottes.

didn't look like she was *sincerely* batting her eyes, but she was batting them nevertheless. She saw me pushing my way toward her, and when I reached her stool, she whirled on it.

"Oh, my God!" she practically screamed. "Dewey, if you tell Mama you saw me here tonight, I'll kill you!"

The muscular bull elephant turned and looked at me, then at Yvette.

"What's the matter?" he trumpeted.

"My brother," she moaned, indicating me. She winked the eye farthest from him. "Promise me you won't tell Mama," she pleaded with me.

Momentarily I thought I had just wandered into somebody else's nightmare.

"I'm not going to tell Mama," I finally said, looking at the mastodon out of the corner of my eye.

Yvette looked at him, then at me, then back at him.

"Excuse me, Gus—I want you to meet my brother Dewey. Dewey, this is Gus."*

He held out his hand, which looked like a calloused baseball mitt. I managed to emerge from the handshake with nothing more than a coagulated pinky.

"Dewey, I just walked in the door, honest—and I was lucky enough to get this seat next to this nice gentleman, who absolutely insisted on buying me a beer."

"That is fortunate," I said.

She made a funny sound. "*Awwwwwwww.* Let Sis buy you a drink, and then you won't tell on me, will you?" She turned to Gus.

"What'll you have?" Gus asked.

"Make mine Schaefer," I said.

---

* I'm afraid the nicest thing I can say about Gus is that he looked like that guy in England who went back to visit his former grammar school with a flamethrower on his back and burned seventeen kids and two kindergarten teachers.

53

"One Schaefer," Gus roared to the bartender. He pushed a pile of bills forward. "Take it out of here."

"I'll pay for my own, thank you."

"Nonsense," Yvette said. "If the nice man wants to buy you a drink, you let him. It'd be impolite to refuse, wouldn't it, Gus?"

"Yeah."

The band was going contrapuntally schizo as the elephant handed me my bottle. By now I needed a good brew, so I chug-a-lugged half of it.

"Isn't the band great?" Yvette yelled.

"Yeah," Gus said.

Gus ignored me from that point on and kept moving his stool closer to Yvette's, as though he was riding a Ouija pointer. He was talking a mile a minute, and she'd make an occasional remark back, like "I don't blame you. I'd be proud of plumbing too." She'd turn and give me a smile once in a while, but I couldn't help noticing the only thing in the bar that really seemed to hold her attention were the three guys in the band. There was a vast dance floor between the bar and bandstand, with so many bodies churning on it and vapors of smoke rising, it reminded me of purgatory as depicted in that same religious cinematic extravaganza where the slave got painted blue.

"I gotta take a leak," Gus announced.

"Do keep us informed of every little excretion," I said under my breath.

"What?" he asked me.

"Nothing."

"Hurry back," Yvette urged, with a smile.

He flashed his ivories, pushed himself off the stool, and disappeared into the mob on the left. I propped myself up on his seat.

"What're you doing?" I asked.

"I thought you'd appreciate the free beers," she said, still staring at the band.

"I have money."

54

She snapped her fingers at the bartender. "Two more."

The bartender slopped two wet bottles in front of us, and I reached into my pocket to get the cash. Yvette stopped my hand and pushed Gus's money forward. The bartender took it.

"If he finds out I'm not your brother . . ."

Yvette began to bob her head in rhythm. She had the artificial mouton lamb coat over her shoulders, and every once in a while a couple of the girls who looked like they'd just been lowered in the Bombay birdcages would burst into laughter.*

"Why do you keep staring at the drummer?" I asked.

Yvette twisted her head toward me with the speed of a bullet.

"Who says I'm staring at the drummer?"

"You're goggle-eyed over somebody in the band. It's either the drummer or that one with the long hair— the one that looks like a fag."

Yvette's eyes pierced me like needles.

"That's my brother," she said.

"Your brother?"

She tossed her head away from me, letting it stop fixed in the direction of the band. She moved her finger through the curtain-rod gesture.

"Your brother's playing the guitar?"

"That's what I said."

"Do you know the whole band?"

"What do you think?"

"You know the drummer?"

"I *sleep* with the drummer."

I lifted my new bottle of beer to my lips and let a good gush trickle down my throat. For a minute I thought I was losing my marbles. Stunned, I looked to

---

* One girl at the bar did look highly respectable. She looked like she might have been a schoolteacher but never had any principal.

the left of me and then to the right. Finally my attention was drawn to the big drum across the room, which had the name of the band printed on it in letters which blinked on and off under ultraviolet light: THE ELECTRIC LOVIN' STALLIONS. My eyes began to hurt as I chug-a-lugged the rest of the beer. I got up off the stool and tapped Yvette on the shoulder. She wouldn't look at me at first, but then I tapped harder. She twisted her head toward me, into such a weird position she looked like an enraged rag doll.

I spoke gently, firmly. "When Gus gets back, tell him both your brothers hope everything came out all right."

I shoved my way through the crowd. Various pieces of anatomy were pressed against me as I went. A fingernail here, an outsized behind there, a hairy arm, a lock of bleached roller-derby hair, an incredible bosom, a red beard. A rhinestone drop earring even slapped the tip of my nose at one point. I don't know whether it was because the crowd was in an alcoholic frenzy or I was in a state of putrefaction, but I had all I could do to get to the street. When I finally emerged, I took a deep breath and almost choked. Somebody had dragged an old mattress into a gutter nearby and set it on fire. That's the kind of thing that neighborhood is known for. If it isn't a burning mattress, then it's a car being stripped or an interracial molestation. The only thing that sort of made me feel better was the sight of the Bayonne Bridge, which loomed in front of me, throwing its lighted arch high into the sky on my right. Every time I see that bridge I think of a teacher in my old high school who was studying evenings for a doctorate in English Lit. and decided to jump off the middle of the span one day, but the dean of men chased her in his car and caught her as she straddled the railing.*

---

* I thought she was an inspirational teacher because she was always urging the kids to reach new heights.

I started down Hauser Street, which goes right under the bridge. You can look up and see the fat rivets and yawning girders. On one side of the street is a huge wall of cement, and on the other, twenty or so cement arches which get larger and larger as they go toward the river. It gives the impression that a pack of fanatic Druids must have worked on the construction gang. I was right under the bridge when I heard that incredible voice.

"Deweeeeeeeeeeeeeeeeeeeeeeeeeeey!"

I turned and watched the artificial mouton lamb running toward me. As it got closer, I spied each of the dangling hands clutching a beer bottle. Her footsteps echoed as she came under the bridge, and she was puffing hard when she got to me.

"I'm sorry," she gasped.

"What for?" I asked.

She pushed a bottle toward me. I hesitated, then took it and started walking. She kept at my side.

"I didn't mean to make it sound like that."

"Like what?"

"About the drummer."

"If you sleep with him, that's your affair. Sleep with a three-titted kangaroo if you like."

She took my arm and pressed against me until my whole side felt like it was being infiltrated with fur.

"I do sleep with him, but not *sexually.*"

"You don't say."

"You understand me?"

"Oh, sure. He's your nonsexual sleeping companion. That's nice and clear."

"You don't believe me?"

"Oh, yeah."

She squeezed my arm as though my sour face was the cutest thing she'd ever seen.

"Dewey, I live with *all* The Electric Lovin' Stallions. All three of them. We have a house."

"Do you mind if we don't talk about it?"

"You're jealous."

57

"I am not."

"If you weren't, you'd let me talk about it."

"So go talk about it. I don't mind. Go up to Times Square with a battery-operated megaphone and tell the whole world you're sleeping with a nonsexual drummer."

"I didn't say he was nonsexual. I said I was sleeping with him *nonsexually*. Don't you understand?"

I refused to answer. We had turned left from Hauser Street onto Morningstar Road and stopped at a stairwell which leads up to the bridge level. Yvette grabbed my hand and tried to pull me.

"Let's walk over the bridge," she said.

"I don't want to walk over the bridge."

"Please."

She wrinkled her nose as though she thought it made her look irresistibly fetching. Actually, with that face and coat, she looked painfully like a constipated koala cub.

"Do you know why I went out with you tonight?" she asked.

"You needed five bucks?"

She frowned.

"Dewey, what you said in your letter—it meant something to me. Remember? You asked me if I realized we were going to end up in a casket soon enough. Remember?"

"I didn't mean the same one."*

"Dewey, we're going to be dead a long time. Let's at least try to communicate while we can."

For a minute I thought she was serious, until I noticed she was crapulously loaded. She kept tugging me up the stairs. Finally I gave in, because I figured

---

* Up until I was eleven years old I wanted to be cremated and have my ashes thrown off the Staten Island Ferry. Then I decided the brain cells might still feel the flames and that a plain wooden box-coffin is the natural way for the ashes-to-ashes routine. I think deep down, though, I want to be quick-frozen and stored.

the middle of the bridge might be a good spot to get a few feels.

There was only one guy on duty in a tollbooth, to handle the cars. He saw us at the top of the stairs, and Yvette blew him a mock smooch. He laughed. When she knew she had an audience, she opened her coat and started running, making it expand like a pair of hirsuted pterodactyl wings. She blew another smooch to the guard, then ran back to me and began pulling me along the pedestrian walk over the bridge. On our left was a gray iron railing—the only thing between us and the ground below. She moved swiftly at first. An occasional car on the bridge would flash its headlights in our eyes, and every couple of minutes she'd let go of my arm and peek over the side.

"Look how high we are!" she exclaimed, looking down at one point where the shoreline was directly below.

"Yes," I said as though it was nothing, but my knees were having an attack of petrified vertigo. I held my empty beer bottle over the railing and let it drop. Yvette let out a scream, as though it had been somebody's baby.

"How could you?"

"How could I what?"

"Be a polluter."

She looked furious as she took her own empty bottle and tucked it into her coat pocket. Finally she took my arm again, and we walked more slowly. Now her tote bag was banging against me.

"Oh, Dewey. Oh, Dewey," she said.

"Oh Dewey what?" I asked.

"You depress me."

I didn't have a ready response for that one, so I let it ride for the time being. I put my arm around her shoulder, and when she didn't jerk away, I figured the move was a good one.

"I'm sorry," I said.

"About what?"

"Sorry I depress you."

"Everyone depresses me." She took a deep breath. "Light me a cigarette, please."

I worked a smoke out of my jacket and lit it, using only my right hand. I didn't want to tamper with the pacifying effect my other hand was having on her collarbone. She took the cigarette, and I lit one for myself.

"You truthfully enjoy carrying a cigarette?" I asked.

"I don't enjoy it. It's a reminder."

"A reminder?"

"Yes."

"Of what?"

"My old way of life, you could say."

She lifted my hand gently off her shoulder, like it was a cruddy pancake, and went to the railing at the point where the great arch of the bridge begins to rise above the roadway. Below were the lights of thousands of houses and factories. The cars on the streets looked like they had just driven out of Cracker Jack boxes, and the telephone poles looked like toothpicks.

"See that water tower over there?" she pointed. "My family lives across the street from it. The four-family house with the yellow porch. That's where I grew up."

"Uh-huh."

"Every day after school I used to ride my bike over the bridge and stop right at this spot. It's the best view of my old neighborhood."

I started to move my hand slowly around her back, squeezing the fur to find her waist. It felt rather like massaging a mongoose.

"It's bad," she said.

"What?"

"Having a bridge near your house."

"Why?"

"You can go up on it and see everything. I don't think the human mind was meant to see so much at one time."

I thought I had located her hipbone, but it turned out to be the beer bottle in the pocket of her coat.

"I had a girl friend by the name of Sue Rautzer, who used to ride with me, and Sue Rautzer would stand here pointing out all the boys' houses. She'd say 'David Bloomer with the long blond hair lives *there*, and Kristopher Kilgoogen—the one with pimples— lives *here*, and Johnny Kollings—the-one-I-really-love —lives under where that sea gull's flying.'" Yvette took a deep breath of the night air. "I used to see other things," she continued, "like that big white house on the corner of the block with the water tower. See it?"

"Uh-huh."

"That's where Judge Barker lived, and every time I'd see his house, I'd remember that for a couple of thousand under the table you could get a suspended sentence for anything short of crucifying a priest. In fact, that whole block I used to call Payola Paradise. In the house next to the Judge was Dr. Sudermin, who padded my father's medical bills when he lied about tripping in a pothole. Next to him was a health inspector, who'd ignore tsetse flies for five bucks. In the apartment house at the end of the block was Mrs. Klugman, who used to be a nurse at an Old Sailors' Home until she weaseled her way into four wills. Two cops lived on the top floor, and they used to collect graft and bribes and scrounge free hot dogs off some poor old lady called Sarina Appelbaum, who had a pushcart in Midland Beach."

"How do you know?"

"Know what?"

"They were *really* scrounging free hot dogs."

"Sarina Appelbaum lived next door to us in the red house with the shutters. She used to have coffee with my mother." She took the cigarette out of my mouth and dropped it in the neck of the beer bottle pro- truding from her pocket. She did the same with her own butt.

By now I had found the fur coat very frustrating. I started to subtly work my hand around the front of the thing and pushed it back so at least I was sure where I was starting from.

"On the block behind us, there was a beer-bellied detective, who used to show up as soon as a burglar alarm went off. If it was a jewelry store, he'd stick a couple of extra watches and rings in his pocket before anyone else got there. Next to him lived a very nice man who was some minor Mafia assistant. Next to him was a Chinese lady who got dressed up like a nun on·Saturday nights and went begging in the bars with a Catholic Charities container. Down near Richmond Terrace used to be a house where the city comptroller lived before they sent him up the river. Some other jerk crashed his Piper Cub head on into that field *there* after taking out a half-million-dollar insurance policy. Pete Pagella lived in that house with the blue roof, and he used to sell graham crackers for hash and bay leaves for pot. My cousin bought a tape recorder from Pete Pagella's brother, who used to work at the docks, where they'd steal them out of crates. And that long brick building right in the middle of those nice houses—that's a funeral parlor they were able to build only because they bribed somebody to lift the zoning laws for twenty-four hours. It got so that after a while when I'd ride up here with Sue Rautzer and after she finished *re*-pointing out David Bloomer's, Kristopher Kilgoogen's, and Johnny Kollings' houses, then I'd start in pointing out corruption, and practically every house had some type of lousy, sneaky, illegal, bloodsucking scrounger in it. The whole degenerate, putrid neighborhood."

I kissed her neck gently. She was staring out at the blinking lights of the shoreline, and she reflexively wiped her neck, quite like brushing off a nibbling mosquito.

"Can you see way over there?" she asked, pointing.

"All those blocks and blocks of ugly boxes they call houses?" She looked at me a second, and I nodded.

"That used to be woods," she said. "Squirrels, possums, pheasants, dogs, cats, robins, blue jays—even an owl once in a while. I had a tree-hut there once with Johnny Kollings, but we never told Sue Rautzer about it. Then the bulldozers came. Every morning when I walked to school, there'd be more and more bodies smashed into the pavement. The cars'd run over them. Run them down as they ran from the bulldozers. Sometimes they were so squashed I couldn't tell what they had been. Little tufts of fur frayed beyond recognition. On Sundays these big fat brokers and financiers would come rolling along in their black Cadillacs to check the construction, and I'd yell at them. I'd stand on the curb, and I'd yell 'Fucks! You lousy fucks!' Then I'd break down crying and be so mad I'd ride my bike straight up here and pretend I wasn't standing on the same planet with them. But then I'd end up looking down and remember house by house, animal by animal—and I'd get so depressed I'd climb the arch."

"You'd *what?*"

"Climb the arch."

I looked at the enormous thick curve which touched the roadway near where we stood. It had two small railings on each side which went high into the night sky.

"You climbed *that?*" I asked.

"A couple of times a week."

"Isn't it against the law?"

She stared at the lighted arch for a long time. "Dewey, let's climb it now."

For a moment I thought I was hearing things. I expected her to laugh at her own joke—the two of us, after a few beers, climbing the arch of the Bayonne Bridge. Suddenly, before I could stop her, she was up on the roadway rail, grabbing the two smaller railings of the arch.

"Yvette!"

"Dewey, please."

Her hands clutched the railings, and she started up. I instinctively grasped one of her ankles, and she stopped.

"There's nothing to it." She smiled.

I opened my mouth and was going to tell her she was mentally deficient. At the same time I was judging the angle of the arch, and the size of the rivets which could act as footholds. I knew it could be done, but still you'd have to be retarded, deranged, desperate—and have hardening of the arteries. If she wanted to kill herself, let her—that's the way I looked at it. I had no intention of putting myself in a position where I might fall off a bridge and get drowned or disemboweled when I hit the water. But then I said what the hell.

I put my foot up on the main railing and eased into position behind her. For some reason or other, with her above me like that, it made me think of Jeanette Matischewitz—the one who used to jump out of my apple tree.

"OK?" she asked.

"OK," I said.

We moved upward very slowly. Soon I began to feel a pattern to the climbing. Right hand ahead, right foot up five rivets; left hand ahead, left foot up five rivets; then repeat the process. I tried making believe I was merely climbing above the roadway of the bridge, that the road itself wasn't hundreds of feet high. Soon we were so high above the roadway, even that was getting me dizzy.

"I thought about jumping off the bridge," Yvette said.

"This evening?" I inquired.

"No."

"When?"

"Just before I quit high school. Because, you see, after I got up here and finished thinking about all the corruption and what the bulldozers were doing, then I'd think about other things."

"I can't hear you," I called out. "The wind and fur coat are muffling you."

She raised her voice.

"I said I began thinking about other things."

"Like what?"

"Plane crashes. Car crashes. War. Weapons. Murder. Torture. I used to put a finger up to my temple and press, as though it was a bullet entering my skull. Then I'd think about The Bomb and the slaughterhouses. I kept thinking of the billions of animals getting banged on the head and having their throats slit. Did you hear me?" she asked.

"I heard."

We were getting very close to the top of the arch. I had to compensate more and more for the changing angle of the climb.

"Does that guy who sleeps with you nonsexually think the way you do?" I asked.

She didn't answer. Finally I heard her sigh. She reached the top and was beginning to slip her legs through the railing. I caught up to her in a minute, but it took me a while to turn and get used to my feet hanging off into space. We just sat there, looking at the spectacular view. A long oil tanker was passing underneath, but it made me dizzy to look down at it. Yvette still stared in the direction of her old town. There was something almost sacred about the moment, something religious about being thrust so high into the sky. Lights burned everywhere, and when I thought of them as church candles, it made a chill run up my spine.

"Did you read about that deer that swam over from Jersey a few years ago?" she asked.

"A deer?"

"A buck. Big long antlers. The most beautiful deer you'd ever want to see."

"No kidding!"

65

"It walked out of the water, right into my neighborhood, and a bunch of kids saw it on Main Avenue. Do you know what they did?"

"What?"

"They ran it to death in the streets."

Her eyes were glistening, and I thought it might be the bleak night wind. It seemed like the right moment, and so I turned her to me and kissed her. When I let her go, there were tears streaming down her face.

"Do you know something, Dewey?"

"What?"

"The world is unbearable," she said. "It's unbearable."

Chapter 8

Needless to say, I did not lay Yvette Goethals on top of the Bayonne Bridge. All I got was a couple more kisses in Clove Lakes Park, between mumblings about what a skunk Sue Rautzer was because she had ended up with Johnny Kollings. And she wouldn't let me walk her home. She just took off into the brush, like a bear at Yellowstone National Park after it found out you didn't have any more baloney sandwiches.

That's my usual kind of luck anyway. I'll give you another example of it. Remember reading in the papers last summer about that girl who took off the top of her bathing suit at Old Barge Beach out on Long Island? All the kids were there for a Labor Day blast, and after that one girl took her top off, another girl did likewise, and so on until there were a thousand girls running around topless on Old Barge Beach.* Remember? Only ten girls on that beach kept their tops on, and they told the reporters who came that the demeanor of their peers was shocking. Well, my date for the day was one of the ten girls who

---

* There was only one cop on the beach, and he got red in the face and didn't know what to do, facing one thousand topless girls. I thought he should've at least started counting noses.

kept her top on and thought the demeanor of her peers was shocking. That's the kind of luck I usually have.

On Monday I brought Yvette in a ten-pound bag of hardy Burpee big-kernel corn seeds. She said thanks and stuck them in her locker. I thought she was a little cold toward me, but maybe it was just my morning monomania. Then she had some nose tubes and attachments to change and I had tanks to check, so she went her way and I went mine. But around noon all hell broke loose. I suppose it started when George was mopping the hall near the solarium. I had seen him mopping the same spot an hour before, so I figured he was stalling around the area because either Yvette Goethals or Helen de Los Angeles was nearby.

"You see Yvette?" I asked.

He pointed to a nearby room.

At that moment Yvette appeared in the doorway. She looked like she was in a semi-phantasmagoric trance.

"Want to have lunch?" I asked her, loud enough so George would start getting the idea that I was appropriating her as my territory.

She didn't respond.

"Is something the matter?" I asked.

"He's dead," she said.

"What?"

"He's dead."

I pushed by her, into the room. I heard George drop his mop in the hall, and in a flash he was behind me. On the bed was a skinny old man with a little smile on his face. I half sat on the bed and grabbed his right wrist to feel for a pulse. There was none. Before I knew what happened George had grabbed the guy's other wrist and was feeling it.

"I was talking to him," Yvette said from the doorway. "I think his heart stopped."

"Hurry and get help," I blasted. She blinked her

eyes, as though waking up. Then she spun on her heels and began running down the hall.

"You can let go of his wrist now," I told George, without trying to cloak my annoyance at his custodial kibitzing. I felt like telling him to get back to his pail of Lysol and Fels Naptha.

"He's going to need mouth-to-mouth resuscitation," I said, swallowing hard and leaning toward the wrinkled, lifeless mouth.

"I'll do it!" George exploded, almost knocking me off the bed.

"You don't know how!"

"Yes, I do."

"No, you don't."

"I read a magazine article on it."

Before I could stop him, he had his lips on the old guy's mouth, and if you ever wanted to see a shot from Dr. Caligari's chamber of horrors, this was it.* I tried to pull him away, but then I noticed he actually wasn't doing so badly. I decided to let go of George and take up the old guy's wrist again. There was still no pulse. After a few seconds I thought I felt a beat. Then there was another. It was very weak, but I was sure of it this time. The more I watched George in this exotic embrace, with that tattoo on his arm going up and down so fast, the more I thought the goddamn bird and *MOTHER* were going to fly off his arm. By now the confusion in the hall was snowballing, and I could hear help on its way. I figured if Donaldson came rushing in and saw a member of the custodial engineering staff giving mouth-to-mouth resuscitation, it'd throw him into such shock he'd keep off my back the rest of the day. George was really doing OK. The only problem that arose was he was starting to do *too*

---

* The old guy's eyes were wide-open, and the thought crossed my mind that if he *was* alive and could still see, the sight of a self-confessed crappickerupper zeroing in for a smooch would be enough to guarantee heart failure.

OK, because I noticed not only did the man's heart start beating again, but I also saw his stomach muscles beginning to twitch.

"George," I said as calmly as possible.

"Mmmmmmmmmmmmmmmmmmmm," he mumbled, indicating he could hear me.

"I think the guy's going to regurgitate."

"Mmmmmmmmmmmmmmmmmmmm."

I didn't notice my bit of information having any effect on George's relentless inhalations and exhalations. His lips were still fastened tight to the guy's mouth. Then it dawned on me that maybe George didn't know what regurgitate meant.

"George, do you know what regurgitate means?"

"Mmmmmmmmmmmmmmmmmmmm?"

"It means he's going to puke," I clarified.

Unfortunately George understood at precisely the moment the forecast became the present. It was an indelible sight—George running out of the room, holding his hand over his mouth, as Donaldson, a ghoulish looking female doctor, and three nurses came running in. They took over, and I just backed slowly toward the door. When I turned to look into the corridor, Yvette was standing there. Poor George was gagging in a sink closet not far away.

Yvette didn't say a word, but I could hear her eyes repeating "The world is unbearable. It's unbearable."

I didn't feel like working the rest of the day, so I kept ducking into the autopsy room for smokes. I found myself constantly daydreaming now about Yvette, and I didn't like it. Realistically I was only after one thing.* All the other stuff I didn't want any part of, although I suspected I'd have to try to understand her in order to accomplish the objective. She seemed to go for the how-short-life-is and destiny routines. I was thinking of going a little heavier on that and maybe even throwing in a little astrology, tarot

----
* A bang.

cards, and ESP if I had to. Actually I still didn't know much about her, beyond her being a broccoli-eating, scissor-snatching, junior inhalation therapist who collected hardy Burpee seeds and slept with an Electric Lovin' Stallion nonsexually—and that she milked free beers.

The sight of The Electric Lovin' Stallions kept coming to mind, too. Her brother looked like he was a fragile lesser angel that just plopped off the ceiling of the Sistine chapel. The guy on the electric organ looked like an athletic frog with its brain recently pithed. It was probably his big pizza-eyes, thick neck, and greasy moustache that accounted for this impression, although it might have been the fact that he was chinless. The nonsexual drummer looked like the Gazelle Boy—that boy they caught a long time ago on the African plains, where he was living and running with a herd of wild animals. They both had that long hair, and eyes that burned right through you.

Around three thirty I decided to kill the last of the day talking to Irene. I had started looking in on her a lot lately. I'd crank her bed up and down. Fill the sugar-water bottle for the hummingbirds. I guess everybody was being extra nice to her because it looked like she was getting sicker. She never really asked for anything. Maybe she'd want me to listen to a poem now and then, but that was all.

"Hello," I said from the doorway.

"Hello," she said.

I went and sat down near the window and looked at the red streamers flapping on the vial of sugar water. She let a clam fly into her spittoon.

"Irene—" I started, then stopped.

"What is it, Dewey?"

"Nothing."

She took a long breath of oxygen and adjusted her nose tubes. The braids were still in place, and she reached up slowly to make sure the bow was still tied.

"Irene, what would someone want with seeds?"

"Seeds?"

"A lot of them. Pounds and pounds of them."

I could see she was trying to give me her attention but was checking the meter on the oxygen tank to be sure it wasn't supplying more than four LPM.

"I imagine it'd be an excellent idea to *plant* them." She laughed, and then had to stop abruptly because it was a strain.

"I guess it would," I said.

She caught my eyes traveling over her bed stand and halting on a freshly opened envelope.

"They returned 'Let's Go Back' again," she said.

"I'm sorry."

"I'm sending it out to another place."

She smiled and looked away. I was trying to think of how to say something diplomatically, but I guess it didn't come out the way I wanted.

"Irene, may I ask you a question?"

"Sure."

I hesitated. I didn't mean to be insulting. I really wanted to know.

"What makes you write poems?"

She opened her eyes, as though surprised I had asked. Then it seemed she was going to answer enthusiastically, but her eyes suddenly became sad. She looked at the tank next to her bed as though it were a dark sentinel, and I was sorry I had asked the question.

"The same reason"—she started to gasp—"the same reason people plant seeds, I suppose."*

At four o'clock I waited on the hospital lawn for Yvette to come out. There was some kind of kooky-looking statue with water dripping out of it into a birdbath. I asked a guard with booze on his breath what it was supposed to be, and he said it was either

---

* You can't eat a poem.

"Buddha Contemplating" or "Venus at Her Toilet." I think he was kidding.

Yvette was a little late coming out. She saw me and acknowledged my wave, but she looked dragged out from the experience with the man whose heart had stopped.

"Want me to carry the seeds?" I asked, reaching for the sack under her arm.

"No, thank you."

"I hope you like them."

"They're lovely."

We walked along without saying anything. I couldn't help thinking what a difference there was between now and the time when she had the scissors peeking out of her brassiere. She was starting to trust me in a subdued surreptitious way.

"Can I walk you home today?"

"No."

"I know where you live."

She looked at me like I was utterly puerile, and then even that emotion vanished.

"Big deal. You looked it up in Donaldson's files."

"I'll walk you home."

"No."

"Why not?"

She didn't answer.

"Is it because of The Electric Lovin' Stallions?"

She cast her eyes skyward, making her look a little like "Buddha Contemplating" or "Venus at Her Toilet." "They wouldn't want me talking to you."

That infuriated me. To think of that guitar-playing Sistine chapel cherub, that thick-necked chinless frog, and the nonsexual cadence-clopping Gazelle Boy resenting my talking to anyone was preposterous.

"Could I stop over tonight? After they leave for work."

"No."

"Why?"

"They don't play Mondays."

"Tomorrow night?"

"No."

"I have a fifty-pound bag of radish seeds."

Her eyes showed the first twinkle I'd seen all day. I decided to make it really sound enticing. "The salesman said they'd yield a thousand bushels an acre." When she hesitated a moment longer, I decided to add the coup de grace. "If you think I'm lugging them to work you're crazy. Since you don't want them, I'll bring them back."

"All right," she said.

"All right *what?*"

A fire engine came roaring by at that moment. She looked at me very carefully while waiting for the siren to subside.

"Tomorrow night," she said.

Chapter 9 *

The house was on Van Pelt Street, three blocks from where the bus stopped on Forest Avenue. In case you've never tried carrying fifty pounds of Burpee radish seeds three blocks from where the bus stops, you ought to try it someday. It's to be recommended if you want a draft deferment based on a double hernia.

She told me to get there at ten o'clock, but I thought that was a little on the late side for what I had in mind. I anonymously called the Bridge Cafe and found out the Stallions started at nine and finished at one, so I figured there was nothing catastrophically wrong with arriving an hour early.

I knew which domicile it was right off the bat, because it was the only one on Van Pelt with landscaping that resembled an acre of overfertilized rain forest. I thought I'd need a machete to get to the front porch. The house was one of those two-story rectangle bores. One of its more cozy and warm touches was a first floor which had obviously been ravaged by a fire. The whole front half of the downstairs was boarded up, and you could see the attractive charcoal

---

* This chapter is rated X. You must be twenty-one or older to read it.

trim around the window casings. The main part of the porch was still standing, and by the light from a streetlamp it looked like a room or two in the rear had escaped the conflagration. The rooms upstairs were lit, so I deduced that was the livable part. I didn't know what the going rent was for condemned condominiums, but I think the landlord of that infestation should have paid anyone to live there.

I found it easier, walking up the driveway. I could see it leading to a roofless garage, in front of which were growing a few unsymmetrical dumpy pumpkins. A big, old wooden cart, which looked like an up-chucked chuck wagon whose pot of chick peas had stampeded, was off to the side, and I was impressed by the fragrance drifting from that area. It was a little like the aroma one would expect imparted by a vengeful cesspool. Clutching the seed sack in my arms, I rang the doorbell with my elbow. After several elbowings, I decided the device wasn't working, and I began kicking the front door.

"Who is it?" I heard a treble inquiry from upstairs.

"Me!"

There was an ultrasonic expletive followed by the pitter-patter of feet, and finally a clomping down the stairs. The door flung open, and there was barefooted Yvette, wrapped in a torn black acetate Chinese bathrobe with a gold unicorn and an apple tree embroidered on it.

"I told you *ten*," she whined.

"I'm sorry," I said. "I didn't know how long it'd take to lug this."

Her eyes phosphoresced at the sight of the seeds.

"All right," she said.

She grabbed the bottom of the sack, and the two of us hauled it into the hall, with a thump. Suddenly my nostrils commenced oscillating.

"Something the matter?" she asked.

"Nope."

I didn't want to tell her the odor in the hall had the

76

pungency of a nerve-gas factory in which chile without carne had just been cooked. She went backwards up the stairs, pulling the front of the sack, and I brought up the rear. Every third step or so she'd stop to adjust her robe. When we finally made it to the narrow hall at the top, she let her end drop.

"Leave it against that door," she said, pointing. "Dickie'll put it away later."

"Dickie?"

"The drummer."

The door was locked with a chain running through two large eyebolts. She noticed me staring at the lock, then wiggled her way toward a second door, which was open. I followed her through it into a large kitchen which looked like a herd of hippos had just finished frolicking in it. Another door off the kitchen betrayed the attractive remnants of a living room whose decor could only be described as Early Hurricane.*

"I'm in the middle of housecleaning," she explained. "You'll have to excuse me until it's finished."

"Can't you do it later?"

"No."

"Why not?"

"I promised the boys I'd do it tonight, and I won't feel like doing it later, that's why. It's going to take at least an hour to straighten this place out."

I glanced around the kitchen and felt like informing her the only thing that would satisfactorily straighten out that culinary chamber would be a fifty-megaton thermonuclear blast.

"Can't you clean tomorrow?"

"No."

"I don't see why not."

"Because we do things when we say we're going to

---

* To be perfectly honest the apartment wasn't the worst I'd ever been in. The worst one was when a girl by the name of Dotti Karpew gave a party at her place because her mother had run off with a Yugoslavian gas-station attendant.

do them. Dickie, Butch, my brother Danny, and me. We're not like other people." She gave me a faintly superior smile, something like a priestess in an Egyptian cinematic extravaganza who has a secret but only the audience is supposed to suspect.

She motioned for me to sit down at the kitchen table, then took off into the living room. I could see her walk to a dirty chocolate-brown sofa and puff up two dirty chocolate-brown pillows which looked so sagged people must have been jumping up and down on them. Then she disappeared from view down at the other end of the apartment.

I brushed some crumbs off a rickety kitchen chair and sat down. It gave me a real chance to drink in the sights. There was an old, moldy gas stove on my left, which had so much grease on it I thought a Long Island Duck had exploded in the broiler. The grubby porcelain sink was piled high with dishes, and there was a sideboard with the cadaver of a Sara Lee banana cake strewn over its surface. I was thankful the cupboard doors were closed, because I thought whatever was in there would be better left to the imagination. There was a small refrigerator that looked like it was one of the first models to replace iceboxes, and a thousand paper bags had been stuffed into storage between one side of it and the wall. Four fermenting coffee cups without saucers were sitting in front of me on a card table. The table itself was covered with an oily oilcloth that was so worn you could hardly make out the design, which looked a little bit like cloud-chamber photographs of yellow and chartreuse atomic-particle trails. I kept eyeing a small saucepan on the stove and a jar of freeze-dried Sanka.*

A vacuum started up somewhere. I decided I'd

---

* A few nice things about the kitchen were: (1) It was nice and spacious, so the five or six garbage bags in the corner didn't crowd you. (2) It had an attractive can opener screwed on the wall. (3) It was undoubtedly one of the better cockroach sanctuaries on the East Coast.

78

better make the best of the situation, so I just leaned back in the chair and lit a cigarette. While I was somewhat transfixed, examining the pattern of attractive stains on the wallpaper to my right, I was vaguely aware of a figure pushing a vacuum cleaner across that part of the living room I could see. It wasn't until the figure disappeared to the left of the frame formed by the kitchen doorway that my subconscious informed my conscious that I had seen something unusual.

At first I questioned my sanity. Carrying the big Burpee bag had probably been a little taxing on my brain's blood supply—because I couldn't have seen what I thought I'd seen. Pow! There it was again, moving from left to right across the living-room rug. The vacuum cleaner was roaring away, but this time I had to admit beyond a shadow of a doubt that attached to its vibrating handle was Yvette Goethals in her birthday suit. She disappeared again, and I decided now was the time to fix myself some freeze-dried Sanka.

My hand was shaking as I ran water into the rusty saucepan. I started telling myself I hadn't seen what I knew I had. Then the sound of the vacuum got louder, and I knew the vision would be crossing in front of me again. I threw the pan on the stove, lit the gas, and rushed back to my seat at the kitchen table. *Urrrrrrrrrrrrrrr!* The vacuum zoomed by the aperture, and there it was—Yvette Goethals guiding it bare-assed. This time she saw me staring. She continued a few feet farther, left the vacuum running, and came straight for the kitchen door. She stood motionless for a second, then nonchalantly came to the kitchen table, took one of the fermenting cups, and rinsed it at the sink. She then placed it in front of me.

"I hope you don't mind, but I always do my housekeeping without clothes."

My tonsils felt ticklish.

"I don't mind."

She sat the bottle of freeze-dried Sanka in front of me, *piiiiinged* a teaspoon next to it, and went for the boiling water. Mechanically, I unscrewed the top of the jar and managed to lift a portion of its contents into my cup. She poured the water and set the pan back on the stove.

"You always—" I started to speak, not because I had anything to say, but because I couldn't stop my mouth from moving.

"What did you say?"

"Do you always do . . . nude housecleaning?" My syntax was deserting me.

"If you had arrived when I told you to, I would have been finished."

She marched back to the living room, released the handle of the vacuum, and started off again. When she was out of sight, I took a sustained puff on my cigarette and became vaguely aware of the fact I was stirring my coffee to death. The sound of the vacuum became louder, and I was afraid she was going to be coming back into view. Two minutes went by, and then I started getting afraid she *wasn't* coming back into view. I picked up my cup and strolled to the living-room doorway. There she was, doing a stubborn corner. She shut the vacuum off.

"The bag's full," she said.

"I beg your pardon."

"The dust bag is full."

She bent down and unzipped the large Leatherette sack attached to the back of the machine. From it, she withdrew a paper bag brimming with dust. She sauntered by me into the kitchen and started emptying it into a garbage pail.*

---

* I have no intention of exploitatively dwelling on her physical charms. Let me simply advance the opinion that if Hollywood ever decides to do a flick about Lady Godiva I think Yvette Goethals should get the titular lead.

"It's one of the reasons I ran away from home," she said.

I put my hand to my throat to assist it in creating audible sounds.

"What?"

"My doing housekeeping in the nude."

"Oh?"

"My mother used to bitch about it. It was one of her hang-ups."

"It was?"

"I could understand my father and brothers—with their stilted mores and masculine mentalities—equating nudity with lust, but I was surprised at her."

She went into the living room and started to replace the bag on the vacuum. It was then I noticed the two-foot-high letters scrawled across the wall behind, pardon the expression, her. The letters spelled out *THANKSGIVING*. She straightened up and noticed my eyes locked on the huge letters.

"That's very interesting," I said.

"*Thanksgiving?*"

"Yes. Does it mean something?"

She looked at me as though I were crazy. "Of course it means something."

"Oh."

She started the vacuum, and then was off again. My knees began to feel a little wobbly, so I decided to return to the kitchen table. I had forgotten my cigarette there on a plate, and it had fallen off and burned a small hole in the oilcloth. Suddenly I heard the vacuum stop, and a moment later Yvette bounced into the kitchen. She pulled open a cabinet under the sink and started rummaging through it.

"Is it *better* to clean in the nude?" I asked.

"Naturally."

She took a pail and started running hot water into it.

"It provides time for body awareness," she said.

"Pardon me?"

"As you clean, you can feel which movements are beneficial. It makes house chores a healthful activity. Did you notice my muscle tone?"

"Oh, yes."

"People only get fat because they muffle the voices of their skin. Clothes pervert the body responses. They distort the thousands of little messages the body sends. That's why everybody's waists usually go to pot. They strangle them with belts. They don't know how to listen to their skin speaking. My waist says things to me when I'm housecleaning. It tells me how to move, how to stretch and bend to compensate for the strangulation of clothes."

She grabbed a sponge from the top of the sink, threw it into the half-filled pail, and headed back to the living room.

"Excuse me," I said quickly.

She stopped and looked at me.

"What?"

"The band . . . the Stallions—"

"What about them?"

"Dickie, Butch . . . Danny—do their waists talk to them?"

"Of course." She seemed amused.

"Do your waists sometimes talk all at the same time?"

"We have regular group sessions, where we walk around just listening to the voices of our bodies."

She disappeared into the living room. A moment later a tremendous blast ripped through the rooms. She had put on the stereo with the bass turned up so far it made my coffee cup nervous. I was dumbfounded. If I didn't have a technique for dealing with dumbfoundedness, I would have really been up a creek. My technique is infallible, but it took a long time to perfect, and the only problem is remembering to use it whenever dumbfoundedness strikes. The first thing I do is say to myself "Dewey, you're dumb-founded." That's primary. Once I realize that, then I take ten deep breaths and concentrate on slowing down my heartbeat and relaxing my body. That calms the glands. Then the last step is I have to ask myself "Dewey, is there something you could do to change your dumbfoundedness to your advantage?" Sometimes a pep talk is required at this point. *"Remember, you only live once! Remember, if you're afraid of dying then you're afraid of living!* Remember! Live your life with a little flash! With a little style!"*

I waited a few moments. Then I walked to the doorway and positioned myself where I could see Yvette washing the living-room windows.

"Hi," I yelled over the booming music.

She froze in the middle of a wipe.

"I was wondering about something," I said.

"What?"

"Do you need help? Maybe I could assist with the housecleaning—that's if you don't mind?"

She went back to wiping the window. For a moment I thought she wasn't going to answer.

"You can squeegee the baseboards," she finally bellowed.

"What's a squeegee?"

"That sponge mop next to the refrigerator."

I went into the kitchen and got that squeegee all wet and ready to go. In a flash I was back out in the living room, scrubbing away like there was no tomorrow. I gave Yvette a little smile now and then. Finally, I asked, "Do you think my waist would talk to me?"

She hesitated, then nodded affirmatively.

I set the squeegee against the wall and started unbuttoning my shirt. I folded it neatly and laid it

---

* When I think of dying vs. living for any period of time, I usually come up with a theory which can most expediently be expressed as "Nature is a rat."

on the couch. Then I pulled my T-shirt over my head and bare-chestedly returned to the squeegeeing.*

"Doesn't it feel better with your shirt off?" she asked.

"Yep."

She moved a chair over to the window to reach the upper half of the glass panes. Actually she was streaking them worse than they were.

"I couldn't find any ammonia or cleaning liquid," I said, noticing that my squeegee was only sort of rearranging the dirt on the woodwork.

"Don't have any."

"You ought to get some."

"Nope."

"Why not?"

"We don't like using anything that'll kill animal organisms."

"I thought I saw you take an antifungus rubbing lotion from the hospital."

"Fungi are plants."

"Don't you kill insects?"

"We had a big fight last summer over whether we should take insect repellent to a picnic at Clove Lakes Park. We decided it was unnatural."

"Oh."

"We try not to kill anything that has a centrosome. That's that thing in the cytoplasm of a cell which usually differentiates an animal from a plant."

My ears were thankful for the temporary silence as the record changed on the stereo.

"Do you think my waist would talk better if I took my pants off?" I asked.

"Suit yourself," she said.

She marched out to the kitchen and started changing the water in the pail. I sat on the couch and took

---

* I've always been bashful about the shape of my belly button. Also, no one has ever explained to my satisfaction why men have teats (tits). I find it disturbing.

my shoes and socks off. Then came the pants and I was squeegeeing in my shorts when she returned. A moment later it was my turn to rinse the squeegee, so I went to the kitchen sink. My knees were still shaking when I turned on the hot water. A baby cockroach was running along the cold-water tap as I gave myself another pep talk. *"Remember! Live your life with a little flash! A little style! Remember!"*

I returned to the living room and was just getting back into the routine when I felt a pair of cold hands around my waist. I let out a scream.

"I'm only loosening the skin," Yvette explained. "You have to wake the cells up."

She turned me toward her and started rubbing my stomach in a circular motion.

"I don't subscribe to upsetting Nature," she said. "About the bugs and animals I mean. How's your waist doing?"

"Oh, it's speaking."

"It is?"

"Yes."

"Good."

She threw her sponge into the pail and opened a closet in the hall near the wall that had *THANKS-GIVING* written on it. A little farther down the hall was a bathroom with its light on and another dark room where I could just make out the corner of a bed.

Ssssssssssst! Sssssst! Sssssst!

She returned, spraying lemon-oil furniture polish on a beat-up wooden coffee table that looked like a Volunteers of America reject.

Suddenly I realized that deep down inside I actually felt embarrassed about standing there squeegeeing in my boxer shorts in the same room with a nude-nik domestic. It was not only puerile; it was phantasmagorically preposterous. Why Life had to constantly thrust me into perturbing positions, I couldn't understand, and I decided that if I had half a brain, I'd put my duds on and beat it. It was nothing but pure cheap sensationalism, that's what I thought. I was being degraded, cheapened, and distressed. It was humiliating, demoralizing, and utterly unnecessary, and I had a good mind to salvage what decency I still had and storm out of that place, leaving Yvette Goethals alone in her nakedness. But then I said what the hell.

Sssssssssst!

"We had California artichoke pie for supper," she said. "It's in the oven if you want a piece."

"No, thank you."

"Lots of nice Spanish onions and wheat germ in it."

"Are the others vegetarians too?"

"Absolutely! None of us has had a piece of meat in months."

"Don't you have meat in the house at all?"

"Nope."

"None?"

"Actually there's one frozen hamburger patty in the freezer. It was there when we moved in, and we left it as a reminder of when we were Eskimos."

"Eskimos?"

"The word *Eskimo* means flesh-eater. Like you. You're an Eskimo."*

"Oh."

I tramped back out to the kitchen and lit another cigarette. I returned, puffing like a locomotive.

"If you'd listen to your body, you wouldn't smoke either," she said.

"My body doesn't mind."

She put a finger to her forehead and flicked her hair to the left and then to the right.

"Your senses are so polluted you don't know how

_____

* I heard that if you visit an Eskimo's igloo, he insists you sleep with his wife. If my wife ate raw fish, I guess I'd want to give her away too.

to decipher the inner conversation of your cells. You should listen to me, Dewey."

"I do listen to you."

"You said your waist has started talking, didn't you? I could make your body tell you how evil weeds are too." She stood directly in front of me, shaking her shoulders like I'd seen her do once before when she got excited. At that time, of course, I didn't know how much of her anatomy followed suit.

"Come and lie down for a minute," she said.

"Pardon me?"

"I want you to lie down on my bed. Do you mind?"

"Not particularly."

She took my hand and led me past the Thanksgiving announcement, down the hall to the dark bedroom. When she flicked a switch, the room was bathed in a ghastly red.

"Lie down," she ordered, taking the cigarette out of my mouth and pointing to a bed on the right side of the room.

"This is where Dickie and I sleep. There are only two beds, so the four of us have to share."

The beds were crowded next to each other, making it look a little like wall-to-wall mattressing. The rest of the space was filled with dressers, burdened with paraphernalia such as Avon after-shave lotion, coconut oil, a deflated Spalding basketball, Mennen foot powder, a chess set, a copy of the Bible, the Koran, a Rand McNally atlas, and a book called *The Recovery of Culture*, hairbrushes, combs, Kleenex tissues, Richmond Valley Hospital paper towels, a scalp massager, a pair of jockey shorts, two pairs of dungarees which had been precisely spotted with bleach, one sock, a can of Aqua Net All-Weather hair spray, a package of Smith Brothers Wild Cherry Cough Drops, Vicks VapoRub, liquid black shoe polish, and a bent guitar-transposer.

I took a close look at the bedcovers to make sure there weren't any centrosomes running around on them. Then I just lay back and put my head on a pillow. That's when I noticed the four-foot-high letters on the bedroom wall. It was *THANKSGIVING* again.

I kept my hands folded on my stomach, and I guess it was my nerves, but the whole bed seemed to be one of those Holiday Inn specials where I'd just put a quarter in the electric vibrator. Yvette sat facing me on the edge of the bed, where the red light on her skin made her look like a sunburned denuded Pocahontas. She lifted my hands off my stomach.

"Relax."

"I am."

"You are not."

"I am so."

"Breathe deeply."

"I am."

"Deeper."

"I'm breathing as deep as I can."

"Shut up." She sat her cigarette on an upside-down cap to a Ponds Cold Cream jar. "I don't want you to talk. Just listen and do as I say. I want your cells to calm down." She began moving her hands gently over my stomach. They crawled upwards like two tarantulas which had received a Nair treatment.

"Eeeeeeeeeeeeeeeh!"

"What's the matter?"

"I'm ticklish."

She flattened her hands so they covered my chest. Somehow she managed to bring her voice down four octaves to a low whisper. "Close your eyes. Pretend you are alone—alone and floating in a heavy syrup. A heavy, heavy comfortable syrup. You're relaxing. Totally relaxing. You're going to let the inside of your body whisper to you. You no longer feel my hands on your chest. You can feel your ribs moving up and down with every movement of your diaphragm. Now you're going to relax even further. You can feel your

88

heart beating, pushing blood into your lungs. You're going to concentrate on the lungs now. You can feel both of them expanding, now deflating. Feel them fill; feel them empty. You've cleared your mind of all external poisoning influences. It's only your lungs you feel. *La da da . . . la dee dee.*"

She began to hum.

"You can feel the tissues of your lungs. Oxygen is rushing into all the little branches, all the little passages, and you feel that oxygen going into the blood, into the delicate moist cells of your lungs. *La da da . . . la dee dee . . . la dee da dum . . .* Now I'm going to bring a cigarette to your lips, and you're going to take a deep puff and inhale the smoke. You're going to inhale deeply . . ."

I felt the filter touch my lips.

"Inhale totally. Deeply. That's the way. That's a good boy . . ."

It began to sound like she was presenting a biscuit to a sensitive Pomeranian.

"You feel the smoke going inside. It's traveling down your bronchial tubes and gushing into your lungs. You can feel what it's doing there. Now that your mind is concentrating, you know what effect it's having on the cells. You feel the minute pain, the little warnings your body is giving you. Your body is telling you to stop. Your lungs feel heavy and sick, and they're disappointed in you. And the cells. Listen to them. Listen to what they're doing. They're screaming, Dewey. Can't you hear them screaming?"

I opened my eyes and propped myself up on my elbows. I could tell by the expression on her face she was anxious for a clinical report. Personally all I thought she did was waste a perfectly good butt.

"Did you hear anything?" she asked.

"Oh, yeah," I said.

"What?"

"Cells screaming. A lot of that stuff."

"Really?"

"Yes. I really did."

She still had her hands on my chest, and I laid back again, just looking at her. Accidentally my hand dropped onto hers, and I pulled it away quickly. Then I relaxed and returned it so it rested on top of hers. We looked at each other a long while. Then she nudged me to move over. Before I knew what had happened, she was lying next to me. Softly she placed her head on my shoulder. All kinds of things started running through my mind. I began having crazy flashes. I thought of Mrs. Konlan and Donaldson and Miss Blotz. I thought of my old girl friend who was incinerated in South Carolina. Then visions of Old Barge Beach, and George, and Snooky, and my father running up onto a rooftop and jamming a cork in a bottle. The letters of *THANKSGIVING* flashed into my head backwards and forwards. I even started spelling *Mississippi*.

"I love you," she said.

I kissed her.

"It's the same for meat," she inserted tenderly, "except then it's the stomach cells that scream."

Chapter 10

When I woke up in my own room on Saturday morning, I felt like I had just been born. There wasn't one thing that could bust my chops in the mood I was in. It was like being dry on the Bowery and finding a half bottle of Thunderbird wine in the corner garbage can. Yvette Goethals! Yvette Goethals! Yvette Goethals! What a beautiful name.* I was so much in love it made any other girl I'd ever known seem, in retrospect, to be a dehydrated Bartlett pear. I kept myself in a luxurious somnolent state, trying to relive everything all over again. Yvette Goethals! Yvette Goethals! Yvette Goethals! I wanted every gushy moment to return. When had she first walked into my life? Was it when I heard her tap-tap-tapping on the one-eighth of a Chock Full O'Nuts office? *"Yoo-hoo. Mr. Thiebold is turning blue. I thought you'd be interested."* And the way she was willing to share her lunch. *"Would you like half a broccoli sandwich? Would you?"* I remembered her gently nursing me back to health in the autopsy room. Subconsciously I knew even then I loved her.

---

* There are only three prettier names I ever heard in my whole life. Those are: Lubidia Lipshitz, Ophelia Legg, and Thynthia Coldpepper.

In memory, it was all so touching. How cute she looked the day I opened the closet door and spied her fingering three rolls of toilet paper. Could she have known then I would love her—even though I wasn't aware of it? Maybe. Perhaps she knew what she was doing to my heart all along. And the things she said on the street. Conceivably her mind was so great she knew I needed harsh words to bring me to my senses. Maybe everything she did was destiny wielding its magic wand. I had been so unconscious I couldn't have blamed her if she had just let me wallow in my ignorance. Time and time again I re-created that paradisaical moment when she marched proudly across the living-room rug, nude, at the end of a vacuum cleaner. The ultimate memory of when she was in my arms was so torrid I had to control its entrance to my mind with the care used with cadmium rods in a nuclear reactor.

She had made me promise not to go to her house on Saturday because she had to spend the entire day with The Electric Lovin' Stallions. I tried to understand. I wanted to understand. Now I felt like plucking my tongue out for having made such a painful pact. *"Yvette Goethals, I love you"* I kept saying over and over. *"I love you."*

Even Theodore and Antoinette had noticed the change in me. In case you've forgotten who they are, they're the middle-class librarian and smog-control engineer I live with.* They couldn't understand why I

---

* This footnote has a few curses in it, so don't read it if you're a preseminary student. The reason I talk the way I do has a lot to do with my father because he curses all the time. He can sue me if he wants, but this I'm not leaving out. First of all, if I get up to go to the bathroom in the middle of the night and the door to my parents' bedroom is open, I hear my father saying things like "goddamn bastard!" I can't help it if I have to go. And when I told him I wanted earphones for my last birthday, he said, "You're out of your ass." But he bought them for me anyway. I can't figure him out.

suddenly put up every storm window in the house without them asking me. Every other year it had taken a threat of disinheritance before I moved a finger. But I was thankful for the toil. It kept my mind busy, although wild horses couldn't stop the memories of our night of love flooding my head. After lunch I exhumed my stereo earphones and strapped them into place while I smoked a pack of cigarettes. I enjoyed each and every puff even more now that I could hear her voice scolding. *"Listen to the cells —breathe deeply and listen to them scream."* Hour after hour I lay there dreaming of her hair falling over my neck. Hour after hour after hour.

By Sunday I could stand it no longer. Electric Lovin' Stallions or no Electric Lovin' Stallions, I had to see her. If she had had a phone, I could have called. As it was, the only thing I could do was go to her house.

When I got there, I thought it strange that every window upstairs was wide-open. Even the front door was ajar, as well as the few remaining windows on the first floor. I knocked gently on the door. When there was no answer, I called. "Yvette . . ."

The door at the rear of the downstairs hall was open, and there was a gurgling sound inside.

"Yvette dear?"

A rough old man in overalls came into view in a room at the rear of the house. He had a water hose in his hand and was dousing the room. When he saw me, he turned the nozzle off.

"What'dya want?" he asked grumpily.

"I'm looking for Yvette Goethals."

"Who the hell's that?"

"The girl who lives upstairs."

"No more she don't."

I guess he could tell from the expression on my face that I was surprised.

"I threw her out yesterday," he grunted. "Her and the three little pigs what she was shackin' up with."

93

I walked down the hall toward him.

"Don't come any closer, or I'll turn the hose on you."

I looked at his tiny ratlike eyes and knew he meant it.

"Can you tell me where they went?"

"You one of those degenerates too?"

"No, I—"

"Ya don't look it, I guess."

"Why'd you throw them out?"

"You come back here and take a look for *yerself!*" he blurted.

I moved slowly to the doorway, keeping my eye on him every second. For all I knew, he might have signed himself out of a funny-farm school prior to graduation.* He pointed to various globular masses on the floor.

"Dung all over the place," he clarified.

"Horse?"

"Of course, it's horse. Didn't you ever see horse-shit before? They kept two horses in here, and I found 'em yesterday. I threw the whole bunch of 'em out. The commies and their horses. Got 'em square outta here."

"Where'd they go?" I asked.

"Don't know, don't care. Should've known they had horses to go with that smelly wagon they had out back, but I never thought they'd have enough nerve to keep 'em right in the house. Always thought the stink was their communist cooking."

I looked at the floor and saw the wood was warped and marred.

"Why didn't they keep them outside?" I asked.

"Against the law. It ain't for animals in a decent

---

* Also, he had a twitch in his right temple which reminded me of Pops—this old guy that lived in my neighborhood, who for Halloween used to give the little kids apples with razor blades and Ex-Lax.

94

neighborhood. I told 'em none whatsoever when they moved in."

He turned the hose back on and directed it to a far corner of the room.

"What time did they leave?"

"Around eight last night. Took 'em half the day to load the wagon and hitch the horses. It's good riddance to bad rubbish, that's what I say. You'd do yourself good to keep away from 'em, mark my words."

Little did I know then that he was dead right.

That night I couldn't sleep, worrying about Yvette. First I wondered if she had a soft place to lay her head. Then I had a nightmare in which *she* was drowning and I was on a commercial fishing vessel that came in to bait hooks with squid and blood-oozing sandworms. I had visions of the police arresting her. It was the most miserable night I'd ever spent in my life. At one point I got up and had a glass of milk and some garlic potato chips. At 4 A.M. I couldn't get back to sleep, so I took a shower, got dressed, and started walking to the hospital. On the way, I stopped for coffee and a stale French cruller, which killed another hour. I still had plenty of time when I got to the hospital. By seven thirty the night shift had already ducked out of the inhalation-therapy office, so I was able to stretch out in Donaldson's chair and put my feet up on his desk. I suppose deep down I was afraid Yvette wouldn't show up at all—that she and the Stallions had vanished forever.

It seemed I had just dropped off to sleep when I heard the metallic clang of a locker door. I opened my eyes and thought I was still dreaming. There was Yvette, putting on her lab coat. I prodded myself, but she was still there.

"Yvette!"

She looked at me a second. She looked worried, and her eyes had dark rings under them, as if she hadn't gotten any sleep. I practically leaped out of the chair and flung my arms around her. She gave me an elbow in my stomach.

"Leave me alone," she said, darting for the small sink on the other side of the office. She yanked a paper towel out of a wall dispenser and wet it with cold water.

"Yvette!"

"I don't want you to talk to me anymore," she said, pressing the damp paper against her eyes.

Now I thought I was hearing things.

"What's wrong?" I asked.

"I don't want to talk about it."

"Why?"

"That's my business."

"Is it something to do with you getting thrown out of the house?"

"How did you know we were thrown out?"

"I tried to see you yesterday. There was some old crank hosing the place out."

She wet another paper towel, threw her head back, and patted her brow.

"That sick hick," she said. "We had to join another commune, and if you think that's a pleasant experience, you're mistaken."

"Where?"

She crumpled the wet paper towel in her hands and threw it into a garbage pail with a thud.

"It's your fault he found the horses," she said.

"My fault?"

"Yes."

"How?"

She leaned toward me, and her shoulders started shaking again.

"You exhausted me, that's why. It takes a hell of a lot of energy to put up with someone whose sensitivities are as primitive as yours. Superhuman strength, that's what it takes. I slept through the whole morning, which is why the landlord found the horses. He comes every Saturday morning to pick pumpkins. He's still got fucking pumpkins growing out there. If I had been awake like I usually am, I could've stopped him from nosing around the windows. And the reason I wasn't awake is you, so it's your fault. I just don't want to be bothered, can you understand that?"

"No, I can't."

Her eyes began to cloud. I moved closer to her, but she backed away.

"We're too different, Dewey," she said.

"No, we're not."

"There're too many things you have to learn."

"I could learn. I've gotten better since you met me, haven't I?"

"There isn't time," she said.

She pushed by me, went to the mirror on her locker door, and started combing her hair with her fingers.

"What do you mean there isn't time?"

She didn't answer.

I went to her and put my arms around her. I was turning her toward me when I heard the *swish* of her hand through the air.

"Get your hands off me!" she screamed as she applied a resounding slap across my face. If I looked surprised, you should have seen the expression on Donaldson's face as he stood in the doorway.

Chapter 11

For almost a week they made me feel like a criminal at the hospital. Donaldson made sure my path crossed Yvette's as little as possible—and he gave me a two-hour lecture on how to control carnal passion by using cold showers and playing handball. Worst of all, everyone on the fourth floor had heard Yvette scream, including Miss Blotz, the head nurse, who now regarded me as Jack the Ripper with a hormone condition. At least the woman in the wheelchair with the wart on her forehead stopped calling me doctor, and I'm not certain, but I think the dwarf spit at me once when I had to change her oxygen tank. The only ones that still spoke to me were George and Irene—and Irene couldn't talk much anymore.*

I hadn't been so discombobulated and hurt since Jackie Kohild did you-know-what in my insectarium. Yvette's metamorphosis was just as sudden and odoriferous, if you ask me, and I tried to figure out what had gone through her cerebrum. That rhapsodic re-

---

* "Let's Go Back" had come back, and now she was trying to decide whether to send it to *The Wahoo Belles Lettres Journal* or *The Christian Science Monitor*.

cline in the crimson bedroom was something very beautiful to me. Beautiful and tender. Maybe for her it was like blowing her nose. But I had begun to see so many lovely things about her that I just couldn't believe it. Then I remembered Maria Montoya from my junior year in high school, who looked like the daintiest, purest young lady in the class but everyone said she was a plaster caster.

I kept seeing the way Yvette's eyes had clouded just before she slapped me. She had been getting ready to cry, I was sure of it.

"We're too different, Dewey," she had said.

"No, we're not."

"There isn't time."

What did she mean there isn't time? She sounded like our planet was going to collide or something. For the first time in my life someone comes my way that makes me feel like I'm starting to live, and she has to say *there isn't time*. I had to see her again. I had to. I know this is going to sound medically awkward, but I had such pains in my chest I felt like there were teardrops in my heart. Either that or camphor balls in my stomach. I couldn't sleep. I couldn't eat. I couldn't . . . well, I was constipated.

On Thursday of that week I was heading home on the Forest Avenue bus when there were a lot of people out shopping in the Port Richmond Shopping Plaza. I was abysmally immersed in my misery, but I happened to notice a face in the crowd that looked like an angelic schnook who had just plopped off the ceiling of the Sistine chapel. The bus stopped in traffic a moment, and I was certain it was Yvette's brother. He was heading toward the plaza.

I pulled the buzzer and got off in the middle of the next block, but by the time I ran back to the spot where I'd seen him, he was gone. I started running in the direction he had been heading, and after I felt I had compensated for his head start, I slowed to a walk and rotated my head like a radar antenna. I was just about to give up when I saw the back of his head. He was sitting on a stool in a Wetson's lunch counter across from where I was standing. I circled to the opposite side of the street so I could get a good look at him. He was stuffing his mouth a mile a minute, and I thought it was very peculiar the way he kept looking to his left, then to his right—like a criminal who had just committed a bank job. I couldn't understand why he was behaving like that until the thought dawned on me that maybe he was in the *process* of doing what he shouldn't be doing. I leaned slightly to the left to see what a confirmed vegetarian eats at a Wetson's. I expected to see a crunchy endive salad or a tempting fruit bowl. If he were really going to hell with himself, maybe it'd be French fries and a dill pickle. But no—he was stuffing hamburgers down his gut one after another. Big juicy gushy dripping medium-rare fleshy hamburgers. Crapulously.

When he came out I followed him into a J. C. Penney department store in the plaza. He went down to the basement level, and because of the crowds, I lost sight of him. When I made it to the lower floor, I looked all over and couldn't see him. I figured he had gone back up via another staircase, so I ran back up to the first floor.

He had disappeared.

Friday, George promised to help me. That's one thing I've always liked about retarded people.* If they like you, they'll do anything for you. Besides, I promised to treat him to an anchovy pizza and fill up his car's gas tank if he'd just do this one thing.

We ducked out of the hospital about ten minutes early. We needed the time to get to the parking lot in back of the hospital and get George's car going

---

* Tommy Toilet-Tongue had been spreading the rumor that George got the way he was because a butterfly kicked him in the head.

because the battery was not exactly vivacious. He swore Yvette didn't know his car, and that actually I was the first one from the hospital who had seen it because he was ashamed of it. I wouldn't describe it as old and feeble, but let's just say that if a movie company was filming a 1920's gangster flick and needed vehicles that looked authentic, I think George could've gotten a hundred-bucks-a-day rental on his jalopy.

For some reason Yvette was late coming out. I suppose she'd been leaving late every day, although Donaldson had warned me in front of her that if I so much as talked to her again, it'd cost me my job. From the car, we watched her wait on the corner of Forest and Bard avenues for her bus. It finally came, she got on, and we followed at a distance. We thought she might have seen us at one point and decided it was safer to let the bus get farther away. That little maneuver almost made us miss her when she got off at Richmond Avenue. I spotted her at the last second as we went driving by.

"Looks like she's heading out for the woods," George said as we parked down the street.

He began fidgeting and took a hand-sized exercise spring out of the glove compartment and started squeezing it. It sort of made the condor on his arm puff up and down, and it made me nervous.

"Do you have to do that?" I asked.

"Do what?"

"Squeeze that thing?"

The Richmond Avenue bus came along, and we watched Yvette board it. Again we were off. The traffic was thinning out now, so we stayed farther and farther behind, but not so far that we couldn't see who got off every time the bus stopped. After we'd traveled about ten miles, George began scratching his head and eyeing the gas-tank gauge. Finally we saw her emerge from the bus at Arthur Kill Road. She walked a long way down a road next to the big highway that was under construction and then crossed over the highway and headed for a colossal Victorian house set on a knoll in the distance. The house was set back from the service road, and a number of towering pines and elms stuck up all around it. It stood out because a lot of the land around it had been plowed.

We waited until Yvette began walking up the wide circular drive that curved in front of the house. When some of the trees began to block our view of her, we figured it was safe to start driving toward it. As we got closer, I could see what looked like a number of trailers and Volkswagen station wagons parked all over the grounds. They had designs painted on them, like sunbursts and flowers and peace symbols and doves. Actually the place looked a little like an enormous camping ground.

"What's that banner say?" George asked.

A huge piece of cloth with lettering on it had been hung from the second floor of the house. It looked like a sheet.

"*Love Land,*" I said.

I saw George's eyes disappear for a second as a sunbeam hit them the wrong way. Then they came back and were sparkling.

"Look at that piece!" he bellowed.

A girl started walking out of the driveway and was heading for the road. At first, I was afraid it was Yvette, but when I shielded my eyes from the sun, I could see this one was a little on the tubby side and had blond hair. She started hitching, in the direction opposite from the way our car was facing.

George floored the accelerator and shot us past the house. He made a U-turn and raced back toward the girl, skidding the car to a halt beside her.

"Let 'er in," George demanded.

I got out, and the girl slid between us in the front seat. I barely had the door closed again when George had us tearing down the road.

"Hi!" he said. "My name's George."

"I'm Beth," the girl said.*

"Where you off to?" George asked.

"Oh, *screw*," Beth said.

"What's the matter?" George asked.

"I left the list home."

"What list?"

"We're out of macro-b's. I guess I can remember."

"What're macro-b's?" I asked.

George looked surprised to hear my voice. Actually, I think he had forgotten I was even in the car.

"Macrobiotics. You know, grub," Beth said. "What's your name?"

"Dewey."

"Dewey? Are you Sagittarius?"

"No."

"I am," George piped up.

"Are you?" Beth squealed. "That's beautiful, George. That's absolutely beautiful." She turned to me. "But you've got Sagittarian fingers. Are you Taurus?"

"Yes," I said.

"That explains it," she said.

"You live at Love Land?" George asked.

Beth filled the palms of her hands with her hair and lifted them above her head. She let the locks fall like tinsel.

"Yes. It's beautiful. I was personally disappointed, but Bob—this friend of mine—and me came in a month ago from Santa Fe—he's Scorpio—we had to get out because he was using the vice president of some mayonnaise company's credit card that we found in New Orleans last summer—anyway this Love Land was supposed to be the grooving commune—your name's really Dewey?"

"Un-huh," I said. I noticed George had already put

---

* She looked a little like the snob who sat next to me in Spanish 105x by the name of Mary Lou Villus, whose California boyfriend, she *said*, was decapitated by a surfboard.

his hand on her knee and was checking it for ripeness.

"Oh, you two are beautiful!" Beth remarked again. "Beautiful. Bob and I brought in grass from Taos—we stayed with the son of a movie star—I think he did westerns—I'm turned on now, you know—it's the only way I can do the downtown shuffle."

A motorcycle came roaring by us at that second. We were going fifty miles an hour, so the guy on the bike must've been doing about seventy.

"Eeeeeeeeeek!" Beth screamed, clapping her hands. "That's my old man. Catch him, please! Catch him!"

"What for?" George moaned.

Beth hugged him.

"He's looking for me. He's got the macro-b list!"

George accelerated, and before I knew what had happened, we were going so fast I thought the fenders were going to fly off. He still kept kneading Beth's knee.

"Do you know Yvette Goethals?" I asked.

Beth looked at me a second, then at the motorcycle ahead. "She the one that came in with the Stallions last week?"

"Yes."

"I spoke to her once but couldn't relate."

"What stallions?" George inquired.

"The group," Beth clarified. "Can't you go any faster? I tried relating to her, but she's fundamentally hostile—I like Dickie, the drummer—he swings—I'm Pisces—I thought she might have a basic infantilism." She started beeping the horn like crazy. "Bob dropped his muffler in Whippany Falls—we're thinking about the Alaska Highway for February—that's a trip!—Yvette's a vegie, isn't she?"

"Yes," I said.

"What's a vegie?" George asked.

"Oh, you two are beautiful! You are beautiful!" Beth said.

She kept beeping the horn as we gained on the

104

motorcycle. The driver finally looked around and started to decelerate. Suddenly he jammed on his brakes so fast we went flying by him.

"Bob! Booooooooooooob!" Beth screamed.

It took us a block to stop. The motorcycle came roaring up to George's window.

"There you are, babes," Bob blurted.

All you could see were two little coyote eyes and a few slightly yellow teeth. He was wearing a checkerboard helmet and sported a profuse black beard, which had the consistency of pubic down after a Toni home permanent.* His shimmering black-leather coveralls sort of made a perfect base for his top.

"Bob," Beth said, "I want you to meet George and Dewey. They're beautiful."

"Love ya," Bob said.

George looked like he was going to vomit.

"Pleased to meet you," I said.

Beth reached across George and opened the door. She practically pushed him out as she slid under the wheel, stepped onto the roadway, and bounded onto the back of the motorcycle.

"Big party at Love Land tomorrow night," she yelled, fastening a helmet on her head. "Can you make it? We'll make piggies!"

"Yeah," George said instantly.

"How about you, Dewey?"

"Sure."

"Beautiful!" she screamed. The tires on the motorcycle squealed.

"Beautifuuuuuuuuuuuuuuuuuuuuul!!!!

---

* I sensed a mild odor drifting from Bob's direction. It wasn't any of the ordinary men's colognes, like Nine Flags or English Leather or Moment of Truth. It was something more exclusive, like Ye Olde Limburger or Armpit of Anteater.

Chapter 12

Saturday, I planned to call George and tell him not to bother stopping by because I decided I wasn't going to the party. I was on the verge of insanity as it was, and I was afraid a debacle at Love Land would be just the thing to push me over the edge. I really felt like I was cracking up—in fact, I was so discombobulated I just lounged around all day on my bed, groaning and wiggling my toes. Groaning was the only thing that brought me a little relief— deep chest moans which moved my vocal cords so slowly it was impossible for me to recognize that it was I making the sounds. Every once in a while though, I'd get up and look in my closet to see if I had any clothes that would fit in at a Love Land festivity. The only thing I found was a deerskin hunting shirt Joey Tesserone had given me just before he moved to Cailfornia, because he had borrowed my raincoat and lost it. It's too complicated to explain,*

---

* Joey Tesserone borrowed my coat for a date with Athena Newman, who had terminal acne and sniffed glue, and they went to a dance at Our Lady Star of the Mountain rectory, where somebody stole it. The next week he moved to Santa Monica and insisted I hold onto his fringed deerskin shirt until he sent me a check in a month or two. Six months went

but I ended up with this ugly fringed deerskin shirt, and I had never worn it. Then I decided to look realistically at my going to the party. It amounted to my having a custodial moron chauffeur me to a commune of love, where over the bellowing "Beauti-fuuuuuuuuls" and "Love ya, babes" of Beth and Bob, I'd be yearning for a glimpse of the toilet-paper thief I loved, while wearing a fringed deer-skin hunting shirt. That thought alone was enough to make me nauseous. If I went to that party, it would be the final act of a madman, that's what I thought. But then I said what the hell.

George beeped his horn a little after ten. I had deliberately stayed in my room after supper and was hoping to make it out the front door without anybody seeing me. Unfortunately, the librarian was at the bottom of the stairs as I ran by.

"Where the hell are you going?" she inquired.

"To a masquerade," I said.

"Goddamn," I heard the smog engineer comment from the living room.

Once I got a load of what George was wearing, I felt better.

"Something the matter?" he asked.

"No," I said.

"You don't like my clothes?"

"No, I like them. I really do."

George was wearing yellow flared crocheted hip-huggers, which clung so tightly I felt like I was being taxied by an Anheuser-Busch centaur. His shirt was a combination of pink-velour polka dots on a background of basic-black plastic, with a collar that made his head look like it was wedged between a set of DC-8 ailerons. The streetlight hit his eyes the

---

by, and all I got was a letter from him, explaining his new theory that radio waves were the cause of schizophrenia.

wrong way at that moment, making his irises disappear, but it sort of fitted in with the rest of the image.

"If we don't get a *Pisces* of ass tonight, we never will," he roared, slapping me on the back.

We left the car a good distance from the house, in case the police raided. George said he had been at one party in Mariner's Harbor during the summer when two cops crashed, and there could've been a lot of trouble except they ended up joining the party and tripping. He sounded like he was lying slightly —like they might have been only subway police or something like that.

"Wow!" George exclaimed as we reached the entrance to Love Land.

"Wow!" I agreed.

We started up the driveway, and our senses were subjected to one assault after the other. The first overwhelming attack was from the blaze of lights—green, red, purple, yellow—the entire house looked like a vulgar titanic Christmas tree. Its porches had strings of colored bulbs draped in wild and crazy ways. Some of the bulbs were blinking on and off. A big spotlight lit the sail-sized flag with the words *LOVE LAND* on it. Some of the rooms were shimmering in ultraviolet, and one of the main rooms on the first floor had a strobe in action, making it look like flashbulbs popping one after the other. Lanterns were hanging in the tall trees surrounding the house, and the station wagons and trailers and carts all had candles and flashlights burning.

"Wowieeee!" George elaborated.

Music was pounding out of a PA system, with several speakers hanging in the trees. Mattresses were set here and there, with people frolicking in various ways—some just laying on their backs puffing reefers and others passing hash pipes back and forth.* A couple of hundred people were dancing to a stomping

---

* One pretty girl was taking a leak behind a hedge.

record as we reached the front of the house. Half of them were on a wide cement court on the ground level, and the others were up a flight of stairs, on the main porch. A floodlight mounted on the second floor enabled us to see clearly, and I'm not so sure that was such a good idea.

"Most of them look like dogs," George remarked, looking over a group of gyrating girls.

"Yeah," I agreed.

"They look like the kind that used to become nuns," he added.

"Dewey! Georgie!"

A shimmering nebula came running toward us. It was Beth, wearing a pair of leotards to which she had pinned thousands of pieces of aluminum foil.

She gave me a kiss, then George.

"Deirdre!" she screamed.

From the dance floor came a six-foot voluptuous siren who moved with the grace and stealth of a Zulu warrioress. She was wearing a conservative green-and-orange-striped sari and a necklace of horse chestnuts.

"Deirdre, this is George and Dewey," Beth said.

Deirdre walked right up to George and gave him a long soul kiss. In case you've never seen a Zulu warrioress soul kiss an Anheuser-Busch centaur, you've missed something.

"I'm in a *bitch* of a mood," Deirdre announced.

"Let's dance," Beth said.

In a minute we were amalgamated into the pulsing mob on the patio. Between the syncopated grunting and chanting of the people around me and the stomping of the crowd on the main porch, the dance reminded me of a sacrificial rite preparatory to the entrance of King Kong.*

---

* The dancing also had a bit of the flavor of the bull dances of Crete, the Hopi Indian snake dance, and the ancient blood-sacrifice ritual where a nude virgin was dragged along

"A real *bitch* of a mood," I heard Deirdre scream again as she and George drifted away.

I looked around us and saw several signs on wooden stakes driven into the ground. They said things like *LOVE EVERYBODY, LOVE NOW, LIFE IS LOVE.*

"What's the matter with Deirdre?" I asked Beth.

"They took her tiger's milk."

I turned my back on the nearest loudspeaker, hoping it would cut down the volume.

"Tiger's milk?"

"It's her hang-up," Beth explained. "She's a Squatter—you know, like Bob and I are Squatters because we live on the grounds and not in the house. People that sleep in the house are called Dwellers—got it?"

"Oh?"

"So she got here a few days ago and didn't know the rules for Squatters—she's a welfare worker from the Bronx—she went and put her tiger's milk in the Dwellers' refrigerator, which is in the house's kitchen —somebody took it—she's freaked out about it—got it?"

"Yeah."

"Groovy."

"Is Yvette Goethals a Squatter?"

She gave me a long affected stare.

"She squats over there." She pointed to a spot in the back where a dark wagon stood. I recognized it as the one that was in the yard on Van Pelt, but now it had a billowy canvas top on it.

"It doesn't look like anyone's there," I said.

"I saw her go out with the Stallions."

"Love ya, babes," came a cry from in back of me. Bob gave me a quick hug before I could stop him and commenced throwing his head in spasms. Now the three of us were dancing, and George and Deirdre joined us again.

---

on her stomach behind a galloping stallion in order to bless the fields.

"I'm really bitched," Deirdre yelled up toward the porch. "I think they've still got it in the *refrig*, but they won't even let me look."

"I make brown bread and hide it with our grass," Beth said. "You can't trust anybody around here. The only thing I leave out in the open is gammelost cheese. Nobody steals that because it's aged by being buried in animal feces for several months."

"Woooooooooeeeeee!" George said.

"Love ya, babes, love ya, babes," Bob kept repeating.

"They accused us of stealing their cornflakes last week," Beth said. "I think Deirdre's tiger's milk is just some type of militant retaliation they're pulling —I can't relate to it—it gives me pimples to think about it."

"Who's retaliating?"

"The Dwellers—the whole place is filled with backbiters," Beth said. "You know what I just thought of, Dewey?"

"What?"

"My father—you know he threw me out of the house because he's a commercial artist and I called him a cop-out."

I paused, trying to put her remarks into some kind of meaningful order. I decided it was impossible.

"How'd you and Bob meet?" I asked.

"It was beautiful!" she said. "I had a room in a whore house—it was a mistake—I thought it was a hostel—in San Francisco's Chinatown*—didn't have a cent so I started beeping the Chinks—you know, skip out on the bill—that's how I met Bob—he was beeping the Chinks too, and one night we were both individually beeping the Chinks when we bumped into each other, so from then on we beeped together

---

* I used to go to the Chinese restaurant down the street from me and have sweet-and-sour pork until they were arrested for killing alley cats.

—we might not go to Alaska in February—I've got an application in to be an assistant interviewer with the Unemployment Bureau—do you like my outfit tonight?"

"It's very shiny."

"Eight hundred and seventy-four Doublemint wrappers. I like your shirt. Looks like unborn mole. Beautiful!"

"It's deerskin."

"Beautiful!"

"I'm *really* bitched," Deirdre inserted.

George was beginning to puff a little. "You think they've still got your tiger's milk in the refrigerator?"

"You bet your beads," Deirdre snapped.

The record ended, and practically everybody else just stood clucking away and waiting for the next one to go on. We moved toward the front steps, where I had to lean on one of the signs that said *LIFE IS LOVE* while I tied my shoelace.

From midnight on, I waited on the porch with my eyes focused on the big oval driveway. George came by at various intervals saying "Wow!" and Deirdre was taking regular flying jaunts around the house with her sari open, and she wasn't wearing anything under it. I happened to make the mistake of saying I was hungry and couldn't stop Beth from rushing off to make me a gammelost and brown-bread sandwich. Actually, looking at the crew that was still agitating to the music, I figured the gammelost wasn't the only thing around that looked like it had been buried in manure for seven months.

Finally I saw Yvette.

First, she was a silhouette coming, flanked by the three Electric Lovin' Stallions. The spot where I stood was well lighted, and I knew she'd see me when she got closer. When they were in the periphery of light from the dancing area, she stopped. She looked at me a moment, then continued on. When they reached their wagon, they lit a lantern, and again they became silhouettes. I waited to see if she would come to the house. When she didn't, I started to walk slowly toward them. As I got closer, the Stallions lined up like pawns in front of a queen. I stopped about twenty feet from their line of defense.

"What do you want?" the one that I had begun to think of as the Gazelle Boy asked. His voice was deep, unemotional.

"I want to talk to Yvette."

"She doesn't want to see you," he said.

I took a step forward and saw his fist tighten. Then I took a step backward.* I looked at them for a moment longer and couldn't help thinking that now in the shadows Yvette really did look like an owl with a thyroid condition. I turned and started back toward the house. Once I looked over my shoulder and saw the four of them still frozen in a phantasmagorically puerile tableau. I halted at the edge of the dance floor, next to a table that had half a fifth of vodka on it. I chug-a-lugged a water-glassful.

"Here's the gammelost," Beth said, shoving a dull-brown square toward me. She had prepared one for herself and was already busy chewing.

I could feel the vodka causing havoc in my stomach as I devoured the sandwich. I thought the food would quell the flames, but apparently gammelost cheese brings vodka to its kindling temperature, because I suddenly flung my arms around Beth and started doing a wild dance. It was unfortunate that the music had a beat like an Indian tom-tom.

"You're relating," Beth said.

"Love ya, baby," I said.

I don't know what came over me, but I started jumping higher and higher into the air. It was like I

---

*The last fight I was in, I gave the guy a black eye he'll never forget. I was in the fifth grade, and at the time of the pugnacious encounter, I happened to have a Ping-Pong paddle in my hand.

was deliberately making a spectacle of myself, and every once in a while I'd turn to make sure the group at the wagon was watching. They certainly were.

"Weeeeeeeeeeel!" Beth exclaimed. "It's beautifuu-uuuuull!"

"Wah wah wah," I said. I started slapping my knees, then warbling my lips to make an Indian war cry. I began to intensely hate all of them—that puny Sistine chapel ceiling sissy that shoved hamburgers down his throat on the sly, that chinless electronic organ-grinder—the whole pack of them. It was at that point that the vodka short-circuited my brain.

"Wah wah wah wah wah!"

"Where are you going?" I heard Beth call.

"Wah wah wah wah wah wah wah wah wah," I kept screaming. Pretended I had a tomahawk in my hands, and before I knew what I was doing, I was charging the covered wagon with a Geronimo battle cry.

"Eeeeeeeeeeeeehhhhhhhhhhhhhhhh!"

As I galloped toward them, The Electric Lovin' Stallions moved quickly to try to cut me off. I thundered closer and closer and got to within a few feet of Yvette before they finally subdued me by twisting my arms behind my back. The Gazelle Boy pulled back his fist, and I thought he was going to knock me cold.

"Stop!" Yvette yelled.

"What's going on?" I heard Beth's voice from behind me.

"Beat it!" Yvette told her.

Beth backed slowly away and then ran for the house.

"Let him go," Yvette ordered.

Her henchmen held me a moment longer, then released their grip. For a moment Yvette looked at me with exasperation more than anger. Then she started to walk away from the wagon, toward a large pine tree in the shadows. I hesitated, then took a step after her. When the others didn't move, I assumed it was all right to follow, but I turned twice again to make sure they weren't going to clobber me over the back of the head with a sledgehammer.

Yvette stopped under the tree and waited for me.

"Ugh," I said brushing off my deerskin shirt. I could still feel their fingers gripping my arm. "Some friends you've got."

She stood looking at me, and I couldn't help but feel a little strange. The way the spots of light now fell across her face—her big eyes glistening atop her skinny neck—somehow it made me think of a female praying mantis.

"Great place." I sat, rotating my head nervously. "One of the better fertility rites I've attended this season."

She let out a deep sigh and leaned against the trunk of the pine.

"You've got to cut this shit out," she said matter-of-factly.

"Why?"

"Because I'm telling you."

"That's not a good enough reason."

She turned her head away and began biting her lip. "Look, I had you over to the house, and we had a good roll in the hay. So what? To us, that's like burping." She looked toward the Stallions, who were still watching from the wagon.

"Our love was a burp?" I inquired.

"Dewey, you don't seem to realize that I'm not all hung-up and twisted, with nothing but sex on my brain. There're a lot more important things in this world, and there just isn't enough time for me to teach you about them. There isn't."

I dropped my eyes to the ground.

"Don't change the subject," I said. "You really thought our sex was a burp?"

"Jesus Christ," she said.

"I didn't think it was. And I don't think there's all

115

that much you have to teach me, that's what I think. Maybe there's some things I could teach you."

"Dewey, it's not your fault."

"I didn't say it *was* my fault. And what do you mean with all this goddamn there-isn't-any-time business? Why isn't there time?"

I looked straight into her eyes as she flipped her finger in the curtain-rod gesture. She looked away, took a deep breath, and then returned my gaze.

"Because we're leaving," she said.

"I could go with you."

"We're going far away."

"I don't care."

She leaned away from the tree, and I could tell she was picking her words carefully.

"Dewey, we don't want you," she said.

I kept staring directly at her because I didn't want to give her the satisfaction of dropping my eyes.

"Why?" I asked, my voice starting to crack.

"Because you're like most people are, that's why. There simply isn't time to change you before we leave, and we can't take the kind of hate that's inside you with us. We can't do that. That's why I had to stop it right away. I admit it didn't have anything to do with us being thrown out of the other house. It had to do with the fact that I thought about you. I thought about you a lot that night after we had sex." Her voice became very soft and gentle. "Don't you think it was a hard decision to make?"

"Then our love *was* more than a burp to you," I said.

"Dewey . . ."

"And there's no hate in me. There isn't. I have a lot of love in me now. I really do."

She stepped back, as though horrified by some incredibly ugly sight.

"You're at such a primitive level of consciousness you don't even see the hate in you. It's all over you." She moved her stare to my shirt, then lifted her eyes to mine. "Do you actually think it's accidental you're wearing that kind of shirt tonight?"

I put my hand to my neck as though I was being choked. She turned and started to walk back to the wagon. Suddenly she stopped and turned.

"What is the shirt made of, Dewey?"

I couldn't answer.

"Were you planning to run us to death in the streets?" she asked.

When she said that, it was as if all the vodka I'd drunk rushed to my eyeballs. The whole sight before me—Yvette's accusing eyes, the figures standing by the wagon—began to blur as though I was looking at them through a fishbowl. I just wanted to get away, but as I turned I fell on my knees. I wasn't hurt, but as I went down, the thought shot through my mind that perhaps I was the deer that was being run to death. I got up and started back for the house. I didn't look back, but I could still feel her eyes slicing the back of my head, like laser beams. Somehow I made it to the edge of the patio and collapsed on a bench. The dancers began going in and out of focus, and I had to look up toward the sky. The pounding of feet on the porch was getting so loud I thought the house was going to fall apart. Then there was a piercing sound, which I first thought was an electronic guitar or a strange horn. As it lingered a moment longer, I knew it was a human scream.

I looked up at the first-floor railing, and there were Deirdre and George with boxes in their hands. They were laughing maniacally and throwing what looked like confetti into the air. Some of it rained down on me, and as I lifted a piece closer to my face I saw it was a cornflake. A *Dweller's* cornflake.

Most of the people on the patio dance floor started howling with laughter when they saw Deirdre and George flinging handfuls of cereal over the porch railing. They hit the falling flakes and sprinkled them in each other's hair. I knew that most of them were

Squatters, and I had to make an effort to lift my head to see how the Dwellers on the porch were taking it. They weren't amused.

"An eye for an eye, a tooth for a tooth," Deirdre roared. She ripped open another box and flung its contents up to the floodlight, which made the flakes look like snow as they fell earthward. Then someone stopped the music, and suddenly there was silence.

A tough-looking bearded bald-headed guy emerged from a group on the porch and started to walk toward George and Deirdre. Deirdre watched him for a second, then let out another squeal and stood between George and the oncoming figure. Then even she stopped laughing.

Finally, the bearded bald-headed guy spoke up. "Are those Dweller's cornflakes?" he asked.

Deirdre gave him a dainty smile. "You bet your sweet ass," she said.

The guy slapped her across the face so hard and so fast that for a moment nobody could believe it had actually happened. George shoved Deirdre to the side, adjusted his yellow flared crocheted hip-huggers, and sent his fist flying through the air. It collided with the bearded bald guy's chin with a *craaaack!*

A cry of approval came from the mob on the patio, but the group on the porch started to hang over the porch railing, yelling obscenities to the Squatters below. One snotty-looking girl made the mistake of dumping a pail of apple cider over the edge of the porch. All of a sudden a crowd of people came rushing by me as I staggered to my feet. All I knew was that I wanted to disappear, because the sheer volume of what was happening made my eardrums feel like they were going to pop. It seemed like it was raining bodies as the Squatters stormed the porch and the Dwellers leapt down like baboons from trees.

I tried to see what was happening to George. At last I saw his head wedged in between those DC-8 ailerons. Over him was the bearded bald-headed guy raising a wooden sign in his hand with the inscription *LIFE IS LOVE*.

"George!" I called out.

I held my breath as the sign came crashing down on top of poor George's skull.

Chapter 13

The first thing Donaldson said to me on Monday was that Yvette Goethals wasn't coming in. As far as I was concerned I didn't care if she *ever* came in.

George, however, was on the job, scab and all. He didn't complain. He acted like it was just a party souvenir, though he did say he'd appreciate it if I didn't babble the details around. As for myself, I couldn't forget the sight of him driving home in his bloodstained, flared yellow crocheted pants, with one hand on the steering wheel and the other pressing a handkerchief to his head.

I hadn't called George on Sunday because I had my own head in the repair shop. Whenever I get a hangover, I squeeze fresh orange juice and keep pouring it into me until I feel better. I don't think the orange juice helps at all, but the squeezing tires me out, so I keep lying down to rest.

"What happened to your forehead?" Helen de Los Angeles asked George while we were conversing in the hall.

"Touch football," George said.

"How's the pot holder coming?" she wanted to know.

"Great," George said.

I left the two of them cackling to each other and ducked into the autopsy room for a smoke. I didn't want to see Donaldson, and I didn't want to see Miss Blotz, and I didn't want to see Snooky. I just wanted to be left alone. But no matter what I did, the name of Yvette Goethals kept popping back into my brain. I tried throwing myself into my work, to see if that would blot her out. I moved tanks around the place like they were empty Coke bottles and zoomed from room to room like a roadrunner. Donaldson even remarked on it.

"Looks like you're your old self, Dewey," he said with a constructive grin.

"That's who I am," I said under my breath.

In the afternoon I went down to the employees' bathroom to hide out. Somebody had left a paperback called *Naughty Jokes* on one of the sinks. They were the most rancid jokes in the world, but I read a couple of dozen, trying to forget my inner torment. *"He sneaked his girl out of the nudist camp because he wanted to see what she looked like in a bathing suit."* That one didn't help. *"He's the friendly type—always inviting ladies up to his pad for a scotch-and-sofa."* That reminded me of Yvette puffing up the dirty chocolate-brown pillows on the dirty chocolate-brown sofa. *"He believes a woman's best measurements are thirty-sex, twenty-sex, thirty-sex."* I guess that joke reminded me of me.

On Tuesday, Donaldson called me into his office. He was incubating at his desk while munching on a cream-filled Devil Dog.

"Yvette called personnel this morning and said she won't be in again," he complained.

"Oh?"

"Do you know what's wrong?"

I felt like telling him she had contracted a bad case of hoof-and-mouth disease.

"No," I said.

"You sure?"

"Yes."

He turned away from me, and I thought he was finished. I started checking how many full tanks of oxygen we still had in the office.

"We expect the one in room four hundred to expire any day," he said casually.

"I beg your pardon?"

"*Expire*. Die. The one in four hundred."

"Irene Schwartzkopf?"

"The doctor ordered an oxygen tent for her last night."

Late that night I was plotzing around in my room and decided to phone the Bridge Cafe to see if The Electric Lovin' Stallions were still playing there. I wasn't calling for any special reason; I was just curious whether they had showed up for work. Yvette had kept saying how there wasn't time and how they were going to be leaving for someplace—not that I cared, but making one little telephonic gesture wasn't exactly going out of my way. The guy who answered the phone sounded like Gus the beer-buying elephant, but I knew that would've been too much of a coincidence. Probably everybody at the Bridge Cafe sounded like Gus, including those molls that had looked like they just came off an unrosined roller-derby track.

"Wednesday's the band's last night," the guy told me.

"No kidding," I said.

"Another group starts Thursday—The Ice-Cream Demigods."

"They any good?" I inquired.

"Delicious."

"Up yours," I said and hung up.

Wednesday, Yvette was out of work again. I had to start doing her stuff, which meant autoclaving a basin of machine attachments and cleaning the machines. The Byrd machines were the hardest, not because they were large—they were only about the size of a six-volt car battery—but they had long plastic tubes, sort of like transparent octopi arms. I was disinfecting the main unit of one of the Byrds with some vile-smelling scourging fluid, and while I was rubbing away, I realized that in the subculture of my brain I was still calculating. Then—I didn't know how the thought came to me—I turned to Donaldson.

"Excuse me," I said.

"Don't interrupt!" Donaldson blurted, flicking his hand at me like I was a gnat. Sometimes he was so puerile I wanted to jam a raspberry all-day sucker down his throat.

"Well, what is it? What is it?" he finally chirped.

"How many *paid* sick days does Yvette have coming to her?"

He looked at me a moment as if I were crack-brained. Then his eyes began to display comprehension, and he pulled out his personnel file from a drawer. Papers went flying this way and that.

"Three," he said.

"That's interesting," I noted.

"Why?"

"She was out Monday, Tuesday, and now Wednesday. I wouldn't be surprised if she showed up tomorrow."

Donaldson *harummmmmphed* and put the file back in the drawer. He slammed it shut.

"Of course she'll be in tomorrow," he said.

"Why do you say that?"

"It's payday," he said.

I let that bit of data seep into my cortex and went back to cleaning the Byrd machine. Suddenly it seemed as if I had just pulled the string attached to the three-way bulb of my brain.

"What's tomorrow's date?" I asked, my voice excitedly leaping up an octave.

"You should know," he said.

"Why should I know?"

"It's Thanksgiving."

When he said that word, it was as if someone had slapped me in the face and painted it in huge letters across my forehead—*THANKSGIVING THANKSGIVING THANKSGIVING!* All the sights of that living room and bedchamber on Van Pelt Street went sprinting through my mind. The squeegee, the windows, the walls, the deflated Spalding basketball, the Avon after-shave, the pair of jockey shorts, they all came scurrying back.

"We won't be getting our checks a day earlier or later?" I asked.

He gave me a stern look. "This is a hospital, my boy. Death knows no holiday," he said pontifically as he scratched his right ear.

Thursday morning the artificial mouton lamb coat was crammed into Yvette's locker just as I'd imagined it would be. Underneath it was the worn orange-paisley Bloomingdale's shopping bag, which I assumed was braced for one final haul. The only thing I wasn't sure of was whether she'd be staying the whole day or just until noon, when Donaldson would distribute the checks from payroll. I didn't know where she was secreting herself in the building, but our paths didn't cross until around ten thirty, when I saw her talking with the woman with a wart on her forehead in the wheelchair. The woman had rolled herself into the hall and was sitting with a huge white-chocolate turkey on her lap. She was smacking the turkey with the wrong side of a serrated knife and breaking off chips from the side. Yvette reached for a piece as I was walking by. She looked at me very, very strangely.

"Make sure you get a juicy drumstick," I said.

She ignored my humoresque, but the woman in the wheelchair, with the wart on her forehead, made a little spitting sound. I recognized it as something she had picked up from the dwarf.

Around eleven thirty there was a big commotion

on the whole floor. Voices were buzzing, and a score of patients and staff members went scurrying into the solarium, to plaster their faces against the windows which overlooked the main entrance below. I figured it was just a traffic accident, or some other crowd-pleaser like that, but after another minute of the bubbling, my curiosity got the best of me. I pushed my way through the group of patients and looked out a window in one of the wards. I couldn't believe my irises.

A covered wagon pulled by two flea-bitten horses was swinging around the oval in front of the hospital. Its canvas top had been reinforced with oval hoops and it had been sprayed with gold paint, but I recognized it as the same one I'd last seen parked in the back of Love Land. Silver streamers and plastic olive branches were trailing from various points on it, and garlands of flowers were hanging around the neck of each nag. Holding the reins was the semichinless electric-organ player, and sitting next to him was the Sistine chapel sissy. The Gazelle Boy was walking in front of the horses, holding one hand on the harness and smoothing his long blond hair with the other. Passersby were frozen in their footsteps as the procession halted at the main entrance. It even looked like a fatal dose of astonishment was creeping over the face of the hospital guard, who probably had on his usual afternoon martini glow, and I think the statue of "Buddha Contemplating" or "Venus at Her Toilet" shook slightly. Another guard appeared and started yelling. He was gesturing for the Gazelle Boy to move the contraption, and it looked like an argument was about to break out except that Yvette appeared and subtly motioned the Gazelle Boy to comply. He slowly moved the wagon out to a parking place on the street.

"What're they doing?" one of the nurses asked.

"Probably filming a TV commercial. Now we're

supposed to find a golden wagon in our sinks," Miss Blotz replied.

"Oh."

"I thought it was Santa Claus," one of the Mongolian orderlies commented.

The whole sight made my stomach feel like it had spent too much time on an icy toboggan ride. I decided it was time for a trip to the employees' john, just to get away from Yvette Goethals, the Stallions, and that entire hydrophobic group on the fourth floor. At least, I wanted to give some of them time to clear out. Yvette would have her check in less than a half hour. My thought was to let them all drive to the nearest Chase Manhattan bank and then into the sunset, to live happily ever after. I was very easily able to reject them, just as they'd been able to reject me. They meant nothing. They were one big sour, decaying zero as far as I was concerned. They were miniscule. They were puny. Microscopic. How I ever could have thought I was enamored of Miss Yvette Goethals I'd never know. She was phantasmagorically puerile.

I pictured how crammed that covered wagon had to be. Besides my fifty-pound bag of radish seeds and the ten-pound sack of Burpee big-kernel corn, she probably had four-thousand gross of two-ply toilet-paper rolls. That thought made me burst out laughing. I was picturing all those weirdos heading for their new world, and they were incredibly overstocked on toilet paper. Then I remembered the bandages, Mercurochrome, facecloths, pillowcases, pillows, first-aid pamphlets, rubbing alcohol, Kleenex tissues, anti-fungus lubricating lotion, feminine-hygiene apparati, and scissors. And that was only the crap I knew about.

The way she had looked at me in the hall when she reached for the piece of white-chocolate turkey on the lap of the woman with the wart on her forehead was beginning to bother me. There was something very peculiar about her eyes, and I couldn't put my finger right on it. It wasn't a look of revulsion. It wasn't hate—not *pure* hate at least. It wasn't joy either, that was for sure. A word to describe it kept coming back to my mind, but I couldn't accept it. It couldn't have been. Not *fear*. Finally I decided that perhaps that *was* the look in her eyes. She was afraid of me. That made me laugh because she didn't have any reason to be scared. What'd she think I was going to do? Sneak up behind her and jab her with an overdose of thalidomide? Was she afraid I was going to choke her? Attack her? Take my Burpee big-kernel corn back? If she thought I was going to make some kind of big fuss over her leaving, she was morbidly psychotic. I had no intention of chasing her down the hall, yelling that I really still loved her. If she thought I was going to create some kind of embarrassing scene, she could just forget all about it. I wasn't going to jump up and down like Quasimodo and call for the cops and start punching and smacking those horses so hard they'd gallop for a mile. I wasn't going to rip the top of that covered wagon off and start hurtling rolls of toilet paper out onto the hospital lawn for everyone to see. I wasn't going to go berserk. I wasn't.

But then I said what the hell.

By the time I got back up to the inhalation-therapy department, I had managed to sublimate most of my animosity. In fact, I was almost happy when I saw the only one in the office was Yvette. She was sitting in a chair, wrapped in her artificial mouton lamb coat. Next to her was the worn orange-paisley Bloomingdale's shopping bag, and it wasn't as crammed as usual. A very modest haul this last one was going to be, I thought. I leaned against the doorway and looked at her. She pretended I wasn't even there.

"Donaldson down for the checks?" I asked stupidly.

She didn't answer.

"Does he know you're leaving?" I let out a cynical, irrepressible, and juvenile chuckle.

No response.

Sitting there in that coat, she looked like an old comic book I read once, called *The Heap*. It was all about some kind of science-fictionish monstrosity-blob that was maligned and misunderstood by society. She looked weird, the way she had her coat all wrapped tight around her.

"What's the new life going to be?" I inquired. "A little homesteading out West? New Mexico? Arizona? Canada? Is that the scene?"

She wouldn't look at me.

"I can just see it," I said. "You get all the way out there and find that perfect little fertile crescent to start building your *brand new world* . . . I can just hear your coronaries start palpitating with all those acres and acres of broccoli and Burpee big-kernel corn."

She lowered her head a bit and chewed on her lip. Then she started humming loudly to drown me out.

"La dee dee . . ."

"Those freaks'll be out in the fields, and there will be Yvette, the great mammillary martyr, slaving in the chuck wagon, whipping up the vegetarian specials for the day—sautéed knishes for dinner, soybeans à la carte for lunch, zucchini with sesame seeds for breakfast—I'll bet you'll zucchini them to death. You'll have your darling little babies from all three of them, won't you? Though I guess the odds are against your brother."

"La dee dee . . . la dum dum . . ."

"And soon you'll have your little community, nice and safe and isolated from the rest of us—no butts, no booze, no fleshpots, no gambling, just one big pack of healthy lovey-doveys."

Yvette stopped suddenly in the middle of a "la dee dee" and looked sharply in my direction.

"Would you mind getting out of my way?" Donaldson's voice came from behind me.

128

I jumped to the side of the doorway to let him by. As he walked to his desk he was flipping through the pay envelopes in his hand and hadn't really noticed Yvette's attire. He handed me my check, found Yvette's, and turned to hand it to her. His lower gums dropped as she stood up to accept it.

"What are you doing with your coat on?" Donaldson asked.

"Good-bye, Mr. Donaldson," Yvette said, snatching her check. "I'm quitting."

She walked right by him and headed for the door. He looked at me, then back at her, and started scratching his bald head.

"Yvette!" he called.

She stopped and looked at him. "What?"

"You're *quitting*?"

"That's what I said."

"Why?"

She put her finger to the middle of her forehead and flicked her hair out of her face. At the same time, she swung her shopping bag so it was facing away from Donaldson.

"Because, Mr. Donaldson, I *feel* like it."

She was out the door in a flash, heading through the passage to the exit stairs. I stood in the office feeling mildly surprised, but Donaldson looked like he was having a prefrontal lobotomy. Then I ran after her.

I didn't catch up until she was outside, on the oval by the main entrance. She was walking in a very awkward manner, and I just assumed the shopping bag was pulling her off balance. The Electric Lovin' Stallions on the wagon snapped to a sudden alertness when they saw me pursuing Yvette—but I didn't care about them. Now the moment had actually come that she was leaving, I found I didn't want to say any of the vicious smart-ass things I'd been thinking of. It was as if we were both about to be put into coffins and there just wasn't time for me to say anything except what I really believed.

"Yvette, listen to me, please," I pleaded.

"Piss on you," she said.

The Gazelle Boy had left the wagon and was heading toward us, with an angry look on his face. There were only seconds left for me to find the words I had to say.

"Yvette, remember that night we shared. All the cells screaming and all that, remember? You said you loved me. You did!"

She broke into a trot. The Gazelle Boy was at her side now. He took the shopping bag and helped her along, but she still was walking in a very weird way. I stayed behind them, and as they approached the wagon, I glanced back at the hospital. The windows were crammed with patients' faces, looking like paper pumpkins made in some kindergarten class, and I couldn't help noticing the woman with the wart on her forehead peering down from the fourth floor. Next to her was the dwarf, who must have been standing on a chair. Donaldson and Miss Blotz had come outside the main entrance and were watching saucereyed.

The Gazelle Boy and the Sistine chapel sissy began to lift her into the wagon, and I couldn't stop myself. I didn't care who was watching. I grabbed Yvette and tried to pull her away from the others. As I did, I felt something hard and inorganic under the artificial mouton lamb coat, and when the coat flapped open for a split second, I got a glimpse of a Byrd machine, strapped around her waist.

The Gazelle Boy leaped to the street.

"Forgive us," he said to me.

I felt his fist hit my stomach and heard the air rush out of my mouth. I sank slowly to the ground as the clip-clop of horseshoes on the roadway began sounding. It was a few seconds before my lungs

130

filled with air again, and with my first breath, I yelled as though my life depended on it.

"You said you loved me!" I roared.

Yvette was at the back of the covered wagon. Her eyes flashed in a way that made me think I had finally gotten through to her, but the Gazelle Boy held her as she leaned toward me. As the wagon moved, she lifted her arm out toward me and burst into tears. She had to have felt something for me. She just had to. The wagon was getting farther and farther away, and I started to stumble after it. They were picking up speed, and just when I thought she would be gone forever and that I'd never hear her voice again, there came an incredible ultrasonic scream.

"I never loved your mind, Dewey Daniels! I never loved your mind!"

I stopped. My legs felt like they had been changed into heavy metal as I stood, helpless, watching the wagon clump into the traffic on Forest Avenue.

I cupped my hands.

"Your brother eats Wetson's hamburgers!" I bleated spitefully, but I knew she couldn't hear me.

Epilogue

It's four o'clock in the morning, and I'm writing this last part in an overstuffed armchair I dragged from the nurses' smoking lounge into Irene's room. Every once in a while I look across the room at her, cranked up under an oxygen tent, her tiny weird bow still in place, thanks to a little special attention from Miss Blotz. She was supposed to die two weeks ago, but she's still hanging in there.

I've stayed up with her for the last couple of nights, and I got to read the rejected poems in the shoe box on her bed stand. They are all terrible, but she thinks I'm writing a letter to an uncle of mine who's an editor at the Perth Amboy *Daily Tribune*. That's the story I made up, and I think she believed it, although I'm not positive because she can't talk anymore.

I'm in a particularly bad mood because yesterday I made the mistake of eating corned beef and cabbage in the hospital cafeteria and found an oak leaf in with the cabbage. I know that sounds puerile, but I swear to God it was a whole big oak leaf. When I showed it to the cook, she said it was impossible. There I was, waving the damn steaming oak leaf right in her face. It even had a little mustard on it, and she's telling me it's impossible to find an oak leaf in corned beef and cabbage. I tell you the whole world is so screwed up it doesn't know its ass from it's epiglottis anymore.

I've been through such a succession of bad moods lately that I get mixed up over exactly what it is I'm feeling bad about at any particular time. All last week I was feeling bad about God making Irene suffer the way she's doing. When you have to watch someone slowly asphyxiating, you really wonder if God isn't vacationing in Vera Cruz or somewhere. Then yesterday was the oak leaf in my corned beef and cabbage and now this morning Helen de Los Angeles had to come in to show me this postcard she got. It was a big long one with a picture of a mud pueblo and a grinning Indian wearing a nine-pointed star around his neck. This scrawly writing said:

Deer Helen:
We're settled in Taos, N. Mex. Thanx for the pot holders. They're selling like hot cakes. People think they're genuine Navajo. We're in the mountains near the hot springs and only thing bad is I got amoebic dysentery. They have a free clinic here. A half million people showed up last weekend for jazz. Another half mil is due. The government is running out of food stamps. They could use a good occupational therapissed too. If we get an address could you send more pot holders?

Yourz,
Yvette Goethals

That made me really feel bad, because I suppose no matter what I say, I thought she might drop *me* a line in care of the hospital. I don't know what I would have expected her to say. "Deer Dewee, Skrew you"?

Irene is staring right at me at the moment. I don't know what's going on in that skull of hers, but I sort of think she's silently reciting her poem. . . . "Let's go back to the summer garden; . . . That summer garden, can't you remember? Oh, let's go back. Do let's go back. . . ." Poor Irene, there's not going to be any going back for you, that's for sure. The only place you're going is six feet down. God, you *must* be in Vera Cruz. . . . Or maybe she wants to be cremated and put in an urn.

And here I am, sitting.

Sitting.

A few moments ago I saw my hand pick up a pencil and start writing.

I want to thank you and the entire staff of my colleagues for all the professional courtesies shown to me, but I have decided that a very important person has crossed my life and gone away. She wasn't perfect, but I must follow her while there is still time for me to come alive. You see, Mr. Donaldson, this very precious and beautiful person is going to start a new world order based on love and peace, and I'm going to be worthy of it or die.

Yvette, I know you sent that postcard to Helen de Los Angeles only to tell me where you are. You're testing me, I just know it. If you wait for me, I'll be worthy, I swear.

Then I said what the hell and ripped it all up. Yvette doesn't really want me in her life and there is no use kidding myself.

So now I'm writing this really puerile resignation that I'm going to give to Donaldson when he comes in.

I want to thank you and the entire staff of my colleagues for all the professional courtesies shown me, but I have decided to return to school and pursue a medical career.

Very sincerely yours,

Dewey Daniels

I don't really know what I'm going to do. It's not going to be that Love Land crap. And I'm not going to give civilization a kick in the behind, because I might need an appendectomy sometime.

But I'm going to do something, and I have a strange feeling it's going to be phantasmagorically different.

ABOUT THE AUTHOR

PAUL ZINDEL has established himself as both an outstanding playwright and novelist. Born on Staten Island, he has lived in various parts of New York and in Houston, Texas, where he was Playwright-in-Residence at Nina Vance's Alley Theater. His first two novels, *The Pigman* and *My Darling, My Hamburger*, were selected as Outstanding Books of the Year by THE NEW YORK TIMES. Both books, along with his recent novel *I NEVER LOVED YOUR MIND*, will be made into motion pictures. Mr. Zindel's plays have been performed at theaters throughout the country and on television. *The Effect of Gamma Rays on Man-In-The-Moon Marigolds* has appeared on television and has had a most successful run Off Broadway. Other plays by Mr. Zindel are *And Miss Reardon Drinks a Little* and *Let Me Hear You Whisper*.